Genetic Engineering

Ron Fridell

LERNER PUBLICATIONS COMPANY
MINNEAPOLIS

Lerner Publications Company
A division of Lerner Publishing Group
241 First Avenue North
Minneapolis, Minnesota 55401 U.S.A.

Website address: www.lernerbooks.com

Library of Congress Cataloging-in-Publication Data

Fridell, Ron.
    Genetic engineering / by Ron Fridell.
        p.   cm. — (Cool science)
    Includes bibliographical references and index.
    ISBN-13: 978–0–8225–2633–9 (lib. bdg. : alk. paper)
    ISBN-10: 0–8225–2633–6 (lib. bdg. : alk. paper)
    1. Genetic engineering—Juvenile literature. 2. Biotechnology—Juvenile literature. I. Title. II. Series.
    QH442.F745 2006
    660.6'5—dc22   2004022764

Manufactured in the United States of America
1 2 3 4 5 6 – BP – 11 10 09 08 07 06

Table of Contents

Introduction

magine inventing life-forms never before seen on planet Earth. Think of corn plants that fight back when insects attack or of goats that give spider silk in their milk. What about bacteria that make medicines for sick people? Pigs that grow human body parts might sound like a good idea. What can you imagine?

Genetic engineers have created goats that can make the same silk in their milk that this orb weaver spider makes.

This scientist uses a special microscope that allows him to make changes to cells.

If you are a genetic engineer, you are a scientist who is working to bring ideas like these to life. In fact, all of the examples just mentioned are real. In laboratories around the world, genetic engineers think of changes to make to plants or animals. They perform experiments to make them happen.

This work takes huge amounts of money, energy, and patience, but it produces amazing results. Right this minute, scientists are working on hundreds of promising new projects. Genetic engineering can help feed the hungry and heal the sick, and may even make the planet a cleaner and safer place to live.

chapter 1

How Genetics Works

The key to genetic engineering is a component (part) of living things called a genome. One of its discoverers, biologist Francis Crick, called it "the secret of life."

A genome holds a full set of nature's instructions for growing a specific plant or animal and keeping it alive. By changing these instructions, scientists can change the way living things grow and behave. And that's what genetic engineering is all about—changing living things by changing their genomes.

James Watson (left) and Francis Crick (right) were both scientists who studied genetics. They worked together to figure out the structure of chemicals in the genome.

Before we can change a genome, we need to find it. So let's get moving. We'll need to shrink ourselves until we're smaller than the period at the end of this sentence. Then we'll climb inside an imaginary miniature submarine and plunge inside a human being.

Once inside, we don't have far to look. Nearly every cell of every person has an identical copy of that person's genome. So let's go inside the nearest cell to its liquid center, the nucleus. Inside the nucleus are twenty-three pairs of rod-shaped structures. The rod-shaped structures are chromosomes. Chromosomes are made of tightly coiled threads called deoxyribonucleic acid (DNA). Separate chemical units are arranged along the DNA threads. Each separate unit of chemicals is a gene.

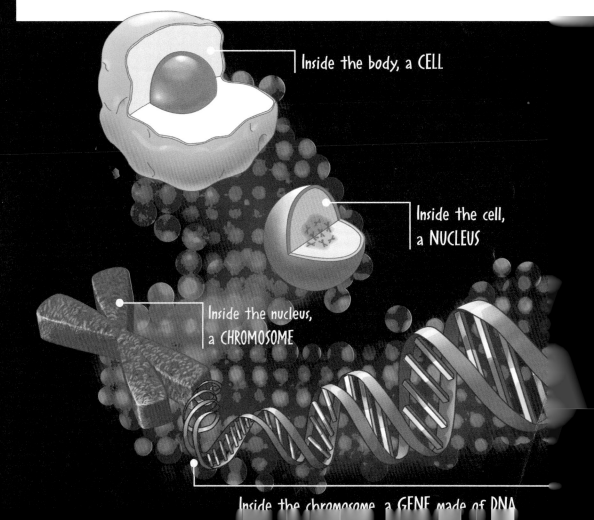

Inside the body, a CELL

Inside the cell, a NUCLEUS

Inside the nucleus, a CHROMOSOME

Inside the chromosome, a GENE made of DNA

This is it. We have arrived. We are looking at the human genome, the secret of life. The strings of DNA have all of the information needed for your cells to live and grow. And the DNA in one of your cells is the same as the DNA in all of your other cells.

A genome is all of the genes in all of the chromosomes of an organism. Every gene tells a living organism how to make or do something different. Genes help determine the color of a person's eyes, the shape of a butterfly's wings, the length of a jackrabbit's ears, how sour a lemon tastes, how sweet a rose smells, how fast a person's heart beats, and everything else about the physical makeup of living things. Genes also affect the length of time a tomato takes to ripen, the amount of milk a cow produces, and how likely a person is to get certain diseases. Genes work by instructing cells to make proteins. Proteins are building blocks that make up cells.

Twenty-three Pairs from Where?

Humans get one set of twenty-three chromosomes from one parent and one set of twenty-three chromosomes from the other. Together, these add up to forty-six chromosomes, or twenty-three pairs. Parents' chromosomes are mixed together in a different way every time they have a child. That's why each person's genome is different from everyone else's, except for identical twins (right).

Same Gene, Different Color

Let's say you have brown eyes and a friend has blue eyes. Does that mean you have different genes? Yes and no. You both have the genes that carry instructions for eye color. Those genes are located in the same places on the same chromosomes in both of your genomes. But your genes call for brown eyes, and your friend's genes call for blue.

To find the genome of any plant or animal, you would look inside the nucleus of that organism's cells. But you would see something different from your own human genome. Other genomes are not exactly the same as human genomes—other organisms have different numbers of chromosomes and different numbers of genes.

Each of these rectangular onion skin cells has a round nucleus inside.

FUN FACT!

In the 1660s, English scientist Robert Hooke named cells after the small rooms where monks lived.

Since the early 1980s, scientists have engineered (changed) the genomes of plants, animals, and even a few humans. Every day we eat food that has been engineered. You may even have an engineered pet one day. Let's look at a few of the amazing things genetic engineers have done.

This goldfish has ninety-four chromosomes!

Strings of DNA

A single strand of DNA is too small to see with the naked eye. But you can see big clumps of DNA without a microscope. In 1868 Swiss scientist Friedrich Miescher was the first person to see DNA. He collected used bandages from hospitals. He took the pus from the bandages and used chemicals to break it down. One of the substances he saw was a white, stringy material that came to be called DNA.

This researcher examines a test tube. The white material in the test tube at right is DNA.

chapter 2

Inventing Plants

ntil the 1980s, genetic engineering did not exist. But ten thousand years ago, people were already developing new kinds of plants. They were farming.

Before people began farming, they gathered food from plants wherever the plants happened to grow. These gatherers took whatever they could find to eat. Once people began farming, they could be choosy. They could select and plant the seeds of only the best-tasting, most nutritious plant foods. They could also breed two slightly different plants together to create a third, even better plant. Such improved plants are called hybrids.

These early farmers knew nothing about genes. But they still selected only the plants with the very best genomes to pass along from one generation to another. The process of choosing plants to raise is called selective breeding. It has the same goal as genetic engineering. It just takes longer to get results. Thousands of years of selective breeding have gone into nearly every plant food you eat.

In the 1980s, scientists began using genetic engineering on plants. Genetic engineers can do what selective breeders never could. They can take a gene from one species (specific kind) and add it to the genome of another, and they can do it fast. Plants with one or more genes from another species are called genetically modified, or transgenic, plants.

In the 1800s, American farmers used selective breeding to choose the best corn to plant.

Peanut Problem

Healthful foods can be dangerous to people with food allergies. For example, some people are so allergic to peanut butter that a single bite can send them to the hospital. Scientists are engineering peanuts to remove the allergy-causing genes and make peanut butter safe for everyone.

Corn That Fights Back

Genetic engineers sometimes create transgenic plants to solve problems. For example, corn farmers have serious problems with insects called corn borers. These pests eat and destroy huge numbers of corn plants. Treating fields with chemical pesticides kills these pests, but

pesticides cause other problems. They're expensive to buy, they take time to apply to fields, and they can harm the environment. Farmers would be better off with a corn plant that can protect itself from corn borers.

Genetically modified *Bt* corn sprouts in an Iowa field *(top)*. *Bt* corn protects itself from the corn borer *(above)*.

Genetic engineers found a solution in bacteria known as *Bt*. Bacteria are single-celled, microscopic creatures that live everywhere on Earth—even in your body. *Bt* bacteria live in soil. They produce a poison that kills corn borers. When *Bt* is sprayed on a field, corn borers eat poison along with the corn plants. The poison stops the corn borers from eating more corn. Then the pests starve to death.

To engineer the corn, genetic engineers needed a way to move the pest-killing gene from the *Bt* bacteria to the corn plant genome. Bacteria do not have a nucleus, but they still have a genome. First, the scientists used chemicals called enzymes to cut the pest-killing gene out of *Bt*'s genome. Once scientists had the gene, they made many, many copies of it.

To move the gene into the corn plant's genome, scientists used a gene gun. The gun's tiny "bullets" are made of metal, often gold. Scientists covered these golden bullets with the copies of the pest-killing gene. Then they fired the gene-covered bullets into corn cells.

Once the *Bt* gene entered the corn cell, it became part of the DNA in the corn's genome. The genetically modified cells grew into corn plants. When corn borers ate these new corn plants, they died. *Bt* corn is great news for farmers and bad news for pests.

Shrinking Watermelons

Farmers and scientists continue to use selective breeding to change plants. Petite watermelons come from selective breeding. (If you speak French, you know that petite means "small.") Scientists spent ten years developing petite watermelons.

After every harvest, scientists planted seeds from only the smallest watermelons. Year by year, each new crop of melons was a little bit smaller than that of the year before. A normal watermelon weighs about 20 pounds (9 kilograms). The petite variety weighs about 6 pounds (3 kg). It first appeared in supermarkets in the summer of 2003.

A petite watermelon (left) is one-third the size of an ordinary watermelon (right).

Rescuing Papayas

Papayas are sweet tropical fruits that grow on trees. In the mid-1990s, a deadly virus was destroying Hawaii's papaya crop. The virus slowly spread across the island's papaya plantations (farms), killing the trees.

Before tackling this problem, scientists reviewed what they knew about viruses in humans. An example of a virus is chicken pox. When the chicken pox virus infects your body, you get sick. Your body has to fight off the virus for you to recover. But if you have been vaccinated for chicken pox (usually by getting a shot at the doctor's office), you can avoid getting the disease.

The vaccine gives you weakened copies of the chicken pox virus. These weakened copies warn your body about the disease. Your body develops chemical defenses against it without actually getting sick. The next time the chicken pox virus attacks, your body can fight off the virus with these defenses.

To learn about the virus attacking papaya trees (*above*) in Hawaii, scientists first studied human viruses like chicken pox (*right*).

FUN FACT!

The papaya tree can grow from seed to a 20-foot (6-meter) tall tree in less than a year and a half.

Scientists have engineered a papaya tree (*above*) that has built-in resistance to the deadly papaya ringspot virus.

In other words, you are immune to the virus and won't get sick.

To fight the papaya virus, genetic engineers created a vaccine for papayas. They used an enzyme to cut a gene from the deadly virus—a gene that would not make the papayas sick. Then they used a gene gun to shoot copies of this virus gene into papaya cells. The added virus gene worked in papayas the way a chicken pox vaccine works in humans. It immunized the papayas. The researchers grew papaya trees from these immunized cells. The farmers replaced their sick trees with the transgenic papayas. When the virus attacked, the plants did not get sick. Thanks to genetic engineering, Hawaii's papaya crop was saved.

Plant Pharms

Food plants come from farm fields. Medicines are sold in pharmacies. A new word, pharming, is used to describe the engineering of plants or animals to make medicines. Scientists want to engineer plants that can make vaccines for people. Instead of protecting plants—like the papayas—against a disease, these vaccines would protect people against a disease.

Usually, a person gets a vaccine by getting a shot. But some vaccines are oral. An oral vaccine is a pill, capsule, or liquid (or fruit or vegetable!)

that you put in your mouth. Ordinary vaccines are expensive to make, and they have to be refrigerated. In poor areas of the world without electricity, doctors don't have refrigerators so they can't keep the vaccines cold. But vaccines in fruits or vegetables would allow people anywhere in the world to be vaccinated.

One group of scientists is engineering bananas to deliver an oral vaccine for hepatitis B, a virus that harms the liver. Then people could be protected from this disease just by peeling and eating a banana. These bananas would not be for sale in the supermarket. Only doctors and nurses would be able to give them out.

Children around the world may one day be able to eat bananas that protect them from disease.

Making the Earth Safer

Land mines are small but powerful explosives that people hide just below the ground during wars. When a person steps on a land mine, it explodes. The person may be seriously injured or killed. A land mine may stay hidden for years, long after a war is over, until someone accidentally sets it off.

Scientists are engineering plants to make them do something no plant has ever done before. The plants will change color or glow when explosives are nearby. Scientists want to grow these plants in areas with large numbers of land mines. Then explosives experts could easily find the mines and safely remove them before the mines hurt anyone.

This soldier defuses a land mine in Bosnia.

Weed and Allergies

Even though transgenic plants can do a lot of good things, some people are worried. They fear that new plants could have unintended consequences. These are results—especially negative results—that we don't expect.

Farmers use transgenic crops to fight pests and weeds. Some crops have been engineered to survive when they are sprayed with herbicides. These chemicals kill weeds. But sometimes genes can spread from one plant to another. What if genes that protect crops from herbicides spread to the weeds? The result could be "superweeds" that no herbicide could kill.

Transgenic foods and drinks might have unexpected effects on people too. Such products as bread, potato chips, pizza, and soda pop all have transgenic ingredients, such as wheat, potatoes, tomatoes, or corn. What if some people are allergic to transgenic foods? Millions of people might become sick. Scientists and governments do many tests to make sure foods are safe, but people still worry that in the long run, the transgenic foods will prove to be unsafe. What do you think?

chapter 3

Improving Animals

For thousands of years, people have used selective breeding to make better animals. In 1791 Massachusetts farmer Seth Wright found some short-legged sheep in his flock. He kept breeding the sheep with the shortest legs together until he had a whole flock of short-legged sheep. These sheep couldn't jump over his fences and escape!

This short-legged ram (right) and long-legged ewe (left) produce offspring with very short legs (center).

Genetic engineering of animals is more difficult than genetic engineering of plants. Animals reproduce by laying eggs or giving birth to live babies. To make a transgenic animal, scientists must change the genome of an embryo. An embryo is an animal in the earliest stage of life—it's just a few cells that will eventually grow into a whole animal. After engineering the embryo, scientists put it into a female animal that will give birth to their creation.

Inventing Super-Mouse

One of the first transgenic animals scientists created was a supersized mouse. To make it extra large, scientists gave it growth genes from a rat. Here's what they did:

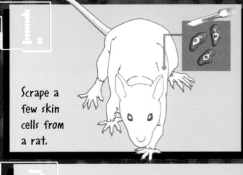

1. Scrape a few skin cells from a rat.

2. Use enzymes to snip growth genes from the rat's genome.

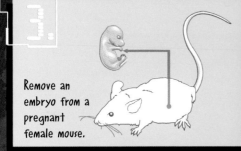

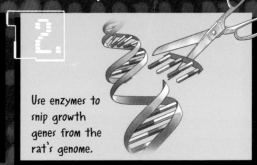

3. Remove an embryo from a pregnant female mouse.

4. Add the rat genes to the cells of the mouse embryo.

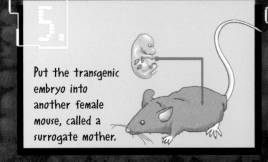

5. Put the transgenic embryo into another female mouse, called a surrogate mother.

6. Wait as the embryo continues to grow. If all goes well, the surrogate mother will give birth to a transgenic mouse in about twenty days.

Fast Fish

Many of the fish we eat do not come from oceans and rivers. They are raised in tanks or ponds on fish farms. Most farmers want their products to grow quickly. The faster something grows, the faster they can sell it and the more money they can make.

For example, ordinary catfish stop growing in winter, when the genes that tell the fish's body to grow turn off. If catfish kept growing all year-round, fish farmers could breed more of them.

Scientists know that some kinds of salmon, carp, and zebra fish grow all year long. So they inserted growth genes from these fish into catfish genomes. The experiment worked. The modified catfish grow all year, and catfish farmers can produce fish faster than ever.

Ordinary catfish (*top*) do not grow all year-round. Scientists are using different techniques, including genetic engineering, to produce fast-growing fish (*above*).

Transgenic fish are not sold in supermarkets yet, though. The U.S. government is still testing them to be sure they are safe for everyone to eat.

Farmers who raise animals must find ways to get rid of the animals' manure, or waste. They often collect the waste and sell it as fertilizer. Fertilizer helps plants grow bigger and faster. Pig manure makes good fertilizer, but it also contains a chemical called phosphorus that harms the environment. Pig feed has a lot of phosphorus in it. Since pigs cannot digest all of the phosphorus, it ends up in their manure.

Genetic scientists decided to create pig feed with an enzyme that helps pigs digest more phosphorus. But the enzyme broke down in the feed, before the pigs could ever eat it.

Then genetic engineers decided to create pigs that could make their own enzyme to break down phosphorus. They used genes from bacteria and mice to create a brand-new gene for pigs. They added the new gene to pig embryos, put the engineered embryos into female pigs, and waited for the piglets to be born.

Fatal Phosphorus

Why is the phosphorus in pig manure bad for the environment? Pig manure is used as fertilizer on farm fields. Plants can't absorb all of the phosphorus in this fertilizer. Rainwater washes the extra phosphorus into rivers and lakes, where it speeds up the growth of algae. These small, floating plants use up lots of oxygen. When the oxygen level in water falls too low, fish can't breathe, so they start to die off.

Phosphorus helps algae to grow in lakes and ponds.

These new transgenic pigs can digest as much as 75 percent more phosphorus than ordinary pigs. The transgenic pigs' manure has less phosphorus in it. Because their manure is less harmful to the environment, these transgenic animals are known as Enviropigs.

Canadian scientists have engineered pigs with cleaner manure.

Silk Milk

Ounce for ounce, spider silk is one of the strongest materials on Earth. It's five times stronger than steel. When spider silk is woven into fabric, it can stop a speeding bullet. But spider silk is very hard to get in large amounts. Spiders can't be raised on spider silk farms. When spiders are kept close together, they fight and kill each other.

So genetic engineers went to work. They snipped out the spider genes that call for silk and engineered them into the genomes of female goat embryos. These new transgenic goats produce milk that contains lots of the proteins that are used to make spider silk. The silk proteins are collected from the milk, processed, and spun into fibers. These fibers can be used to make extremely strong but lightweight cloth. One day soldiers may actually wear bulletproof vests made from spider silk!

FUN FACT!

The toughest spider silk is the dragline silk from the orb weaver spider. Dragline silk must support a spider's weight, so it is the strongest silk a spider makes.

Some animal genetic engineering projects sound more like science fiction than science fact. In the United States, patients have to wait for months or even years to get an organ transplant. Scientists would like to supply healthy new organs, such as hearts, lungs, kidneys, and livers, to all people who need them.

One experiment is engineering pigs to produce human body parts. Scientists have engineered the genomes of these pigs so that their organs are more like human organs. They hope that human bodies will accept these new body parts. But scientists still have a lot more experimenting to do before they will be ready to replace human organs with pig organs.

Humans who need new hearts must have another human heart (above) transplanted into their bodies. One day, pig hearts instead of human hearts may be transplanted into humans.

Fun Fish

Not all transgenic animals solve a problem. Some are used just for fun. One example is a transgenic zebra fish that glows in the dark. It was originally invented to help detect pollution by glowing only in polluted water. But by accident, a scientist created several varieties of fish that glow all the time. The glow comes from the genes of other sea creatures. Zebra fish with a sea anemone gene glow red. Those with a jellyfish gene glow green.

Fluorescent genes make these small fish shimmer and glow in the dark like neon signs. They are sold under brand names such as "GloFish," "Night Light Fish," and "Night Pearls." They are the world's first transgenic house pets.

Genetic engineers have created zebra fish that glow.

Cloning Animals

Scientists have invented another new kind of animal, a clone. Animal cloning is not truly genetic engineering. Scientists don't change the animal's genome. But cloning uses many of the same tools and methods as genetic engineering.

What makes a clone different from other animals? Most of the time, an animal has two parents. Its genome is a mixture of genes from its mother and its father. But a clone's genome is an exact copy of the genome of only one parent.

Why clone animals? Imagine if you could clone copies of your very best dairy cow, the one that gives the most and best milk. Or the pig that produces the best pork.

Dolly, the first cloned sheep, lived from 1996 to 2003.

Or the sheep in your flock that produces the very best wool. Then every animal you owned would be the very best of its kind.

The very first cloned mammal was Dolly the sheep. She was born in 1996. A team of scientists from Scotland cloned her from an adult female sheep.

Hello, Dolly

See if you can answer this question: Which of the sheep (#1, #2, or #3) is Dolly's parent?

Step 1
Scientists took an egg from the uterus of sheep #1 and removed the egg's nucleus, leaving the egg empty.

Step 2
Scientists took a cell from the udder of sheep #2 and removed its nucleus.

Step 3
They inserted the nucleus from sheep #2 into the empty egg of sheep #1.

Step 4
They put this egg inside sheep #3.

Step 5
Inside sheep #3, the egg grew into an embryo and finally a baby sheep named Dolly was born.

Dolly is a clone of sheep #2 because sheep #2 supplied the nucleus that contained Dolly's genome.

Unintended Consequences

Some people fear that creating transgenic animals will have unintended consequences. They worry that the animals may not turn out exactly as planned. But other people argue that genetic engineering has the same result as selective breeding—only faster.

Genetic engineers want to eliminate malaria, a virus carried by mosquitoes that kills millions of people each year. Scientists are trying to engineer mosquitoes that resist the virus. Insects that don't carry the virus can't pass it on to humans. Scientists hope to release thousands of engineered mosquitoes into the wild, where they can breed with other mosquitoes. If all goes well, the antimalaria genes will spread through the whole mosquito population, and malaria will be conquered.

Hold on a minute, say people who worry about genetic engineering. What if these transgenic mosquitoes carry other diseases that we don't even know about yet? Then we may create worse problems than the one we solve.

Genetically engineered animals, including mosquitoes and salmon, raise concerns.

Some people have the same kinds of worries about "supersalmon." These transgenic salmon are engineered to grow larger than ordinary salmon. They are raised on fish farms and have never been in the wild. But suppose they escape into rivers and oceans and breed with wild salmon? Transgenic salmon have never had to fight off predators and hunt their own food. This new breed of transgenic-wild salmon may not be able to survive in the wild. Then the entire supply of wild salmon could be killed off. What do you think?

chapter 4

Engineering People

The human genome has more than twenty thousand genes. Your genome holds all the instructions for making your body and keeping it running. No one is born with a perfect genome. Everyone has some genes that don't work as well as they should. These are called faulty genes. As people get older, more faulty genes show up.

Your body has trillions of cells. A trillion is a million million. Every day, old cells die and new ones replace them. Each

These human skin cells, shown through a microscope, have been stained with dye to make their structures visible.

new cell is supposed to have the exact same copy of the genome. But sometimes things go wrong. A gene doesn't get copied exactly right. These mistakes are called mutations.

Most mutations are harmless. Some even help make living things healthier and stronger. But sometimes harmful mutations show up. Some mutations cause deadly diseases. For example, one mutation causes the disease severe combined immunodeficiency (SCID). This condition makes people unable to fight off ordinary colds and other infections. These infections can kill them.

To cure diseases like SCID, scientists have recently started using genetic engineering to repair faulty genes. Doctors and genetic researchers are learning how to get into human genomes and replace damaged genes with healthy ones. This is known as gene therapy.

Ashanthi DeSilva (*right*) and Cynthia Cutshall (*left*) were the first two people ever to receive gene therapy.

Viruses That Help

In gene therapy, scientists do a lot of the same things they do to create transgenic plants and animals. But the human genome is harder to engineer. Most of the time, scientists want to change the genome of a person who has already been born. The trickiest part of gene therapy is delivering engineered genes to the genome.

Scientists sometimes use viruses for delivering genes. Scientists know how to disable, or weaken, viruses. They get rid of the parts of a virus that cause sickness. Scientists then put healthy genes into the disabled viruses. Then the viruses can deliver the healthy genes into the genome. If all goes well, the healthy genes replace the faulty genes and the patient is cured. This type of therapy has been used to help SCID patients.

Stem Cells to the Rescue

Your body has different types of tissues, such as muscle, lung, skin, and heart. Each tissue type has its own special repair crew of cells called adult stem cells. (Even in newborn babies, these cells are called adult stem cells.) For example, when you cut your finger, your body sends out a crew of skin stem cells. This repair crew travels to the cut and makes new skin to heal it.

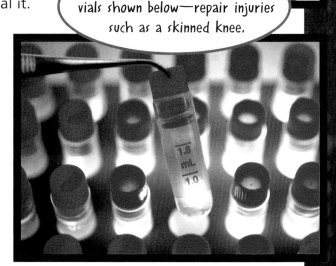

Stem cells—contained in the vials shown below—repair injuries such as a skinned knee.

These repair crews can't always handle the job when a person is very sick. Someone with heart disease, for instance, might need a huge supply of heart cells to repair the damage—more than the stem cell repair crews can possibly supply.

In a case like this, scientists are hoping that it will be possible to take a few heart stem cells from the patient and clone, or copy, them. They would inject many copies back into the patient. With more stem cells, the patient's body would be able to do a better job of healing itself.

FUN FACT!
Your body makes new skin cells all the time. You shed your skin, little by little, every thirty-five days. That means you grow a completely new skin about ten times a year!

Scientists also believe they could make stem cells grow into whole body parts. Instead of using pigs to make human organs, scientists could grow human organs from human stem cells. In a laboratory, scientists would take stem cells from a patient and use them to make all of the cells of a new organ. Doing this would help people who need organ transplants. It could also help healthy people live longer. As people grow older, their organs naturally wear out. Before they do, the old organs could be replaced with brand-new ones grown from stem cells.

Naked Mice for Sale!

Laboratories supply different kinds of mice to scientists for research. One variety is known as a nude mouse (below). The genes that tell the mouse's body how to grow hair are missing from its genome.

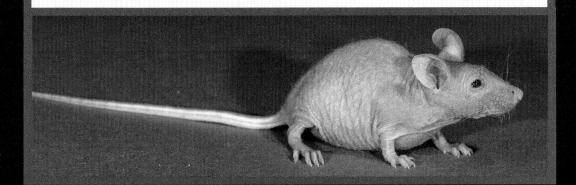

Going against Nature?

People who worry about genetic engineering worry the most about engineering humans. Some people believe that genetic engineering is too risky to try on humans.

For example, patients with SCID have been helped by gene therapy. But two French boys with SCID who were being treated with gene therapy came down with leukemia, or cancer of the blood. The boys' cancer was successfully treated, but it worried scientists. Scientists believe that the gene used to make the boys healthy ended up in the wrong part of their genome and that this caused the leukemia. When the two boys became sick, other genetic engineering experiments around the world were stopped.

Some people object to gene therapy and growing human organs in animals because scientists don't know enough about how the human genome works. These people say we should wait until we know more. Other people object because they believe changing genomes goes against nature. Human and animal genomes were not meant to be invaded by scientists and changed, they argue. What do you think?

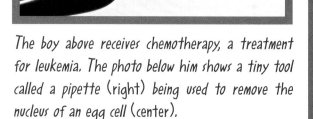

The boy above receives chemotherapy, a treatment for leukemia. The photo below him shows a tiny tool called a pipette (right) being used to remove the nucleus of an egg cell (center).

Knockout Mice

Scientists have a lot to learn about the part that each gene plays in the human body. Laboratory experiments on people can be very dangerous. If an experiment on a person did not work as expected, the person could suffer and die. So to learn more, scientists experiment on animals.

Mice are popular lab animals. They are easy to handle, they reproduce quickly, and they have many of the same genes that humans have. To test different genes, scientists go into the genome of a mouse embryo and knock out, or turn off, a specific gene. The mouse is called a knockout mouse. Once it is born, researchers watch closely to see how the mouse is different from mice that are not missing the gene. These experiments teach scientists what part the knocked-out gene plays in growing and running the body.

Mice have a lot in common with humans, even though they have forty chromosomes and humans have forty-six.

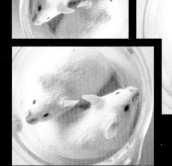

FUN FACT!

One female mouse can have more than one hundred babies in one year.

chapter 5

Looking to the Future

Genetic engineering has the potential to change our lives in many different ways. Let's look at some of the wildest ideas that genetic engineers hope to bring to life in the future.

Blue Roses

Roses are red. They are also pink, yellow, white, and purple. But roses are not blue—not yet. Many people want to be able to buy blue roses and grow them in their gardens. No one has ever been able to breed a blue rose. But genetic engineering may change this.

Roses come in hundreds of varieties and colors, but none of them are blue.

Companies that sell flowers have spent millions of dollars to engineer a blue rose. Scientists have tried engineering genes from blue petunias and other flowers into rose genomes. So far the results are disappointing—and purple. But the company that can create blue roses will make lots of money. So scientists will keep trying to engineer them.

Engineered Pets

Are you allergic to cats? Many people are. People with this allergy suffer itchy eyes, scratchy throats, runny noses, and violent sneezing when they are around cats. But some of these people love cats and wish they could have one for a pet.

Scientists have found the cat genes that make people allergic to cats. Tests show that cats could live normal, healthy lives if these genes were engineered out of their genome. Scientists are trying to engineer allergy-free cats to sell in the United States and Japan.

Nonallergenic cats would likely be created by cloning. The cats above are two of the world's first cloned cats.

Members of animal rights groups (organizations that work to prevent cruelty to animals) say the tests scientists perform will harm cats and kittens. They fear that too many animals will be harmed to make the results worthwhile.

Healthy Couch Potatoes

Scientists have engineered mice to be terrific long-distance runners. The key is "fat-switch" genes. When fat-switch genes are turned on—in mice or in people—the body burns fat. Scientists have engineered mice so their fat-switch genes are always turned on. This gives them a constant supply of energy. The engineers tested the mice by having them run on treadmills. The "marathon mice" could run nearly twice as far as other mice before stopping.

Someday, scientists say, they may be able to engineer people the same way. With their fat-switch genes turned on all the time, some people might turn into super marathon runners, just like the mice.

But this is not why scientists have engineered fat-switch genes. They want to help people lose weight. The engineered mice stay thin even when they eat only high-fat foods and don't exercise. Their fat-switch genes keep the mice's bodies burning fat even when they're fast asleep!

Scientists use exercise wheels to test how long mice

Super Baby

Picture a four-year-old boy holding a 7-pound (3 kg) weight in each hand while holding his arms straight out at his sides. Many full-grown adults aren't strong enough to do this. The boy, who lives in Germany, has a rare genetic mutation that keeps his myostatin gene permanently switched off. Myostatin is a protein that limits muscle growth. So the boy has twice the muscle of other kids his age and only half the body fat. A rare breed of cattle, Belgian Blue, has the same kind of mutation. These powerful cattle have bulging muscles all over their bodies and hardly any fat.

Researchers are working on gene therapy treatments for humans based on this mutation. They want to engineer people so that their myostatin gene is switched off. But they don't want to create more superstrong people.

Adult male Belgian Blue cattle, like the one shown below, weigh approximately 2,700 pounds (1,200 kg).

They want to treat people who have muscular dystrophy. This disease weakens muscles and can cripple the bodies of children and adults. With the myostatin gene switched off, people with muscular dystrophy might be able to repair their own damaged muscles.

Cures from Chips

You've heard of computer memory chips. These tiny slivers store huge amounts of information. Recently scientists have created tiny glass gene chips for storing information about diseases. A doctor can take a sample of a patient's cells and coat the gene chip with them. A single chip shows all the patient's genes. When a gene is switched on, it lights up on the chip.

These images show gene chips. The areas of the chip that light up indicate genes that are switched on.

The chip gives a picture of a patient's genome. If the scientists know that a patient has a certain disease, they can compare the gene chip with the gene chips of many patients who have the same disease. Then scientists can identify which genes may be causing the disease. They can work on designing medicines and gene therapy treatments for patients.

Designer Babies

Imagine that we know how to engineer embryos to produce "perfect" children. Parents could walk into a doctor's office and design the genome of their child-to-be. Let's say their idea of a perfect child is a girl with black hair and brown eyes who will be 5 feet 10 inches (1.8 meters) tall when she's an adult. They want her to have special talents for doing math and playing the piano. And they think her personality should be just a little shy.

IVF

Scientists may still be years away from creating designer babies or human clones, but they have already figured out one important piece of that puzzle. In vitro fertilization (IVF) was developed in the 1970s to help infertile couples have children. Scientists use a couple's eggs and sperm to grow embryos in lab dishes. Some of these embryos are placed inside a woman to grow into a baby. IVF has resulted in the birth of more than one million babies worldwide.

As part of in vitro fertilization, a pipette containing sperm (left) is inserted into a human egg cell (right).

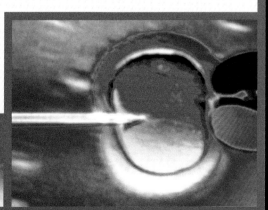

Whoa, Not So Fast!

Many people oppose genetic engineering. They say scientists are moving much too quickly. They believe that scientists don't know enough about genomes yet to be sure their work won't end up doing more harm than good.

This goes for engineering plants and animals as well as humans. Opponents admit that, so far, no transgenic plant or animal has harmed anyone. But no matter how careful we think we are, they say, it may not be careful enough.

Other people, including many scientists, disagree—sort of. No one says that nothing bad could ever happen. Scientific studies warn that transgenic plants and animals will likely bring surprises in the future. And some of these surprises may bring problems. But that's how it is with anything new, these people say. We can never be totally sure that a new technology is completely safe. We must use it, see what happens, and keep an eye out for unintended consequences. We must move ahead with the genetic engineering of plants and animals, they say—but cautiously. What do you think?

A researcher examines genetically modified corn (top). Protesters in Germany (above) want their government to prohibit genetically modified food.

Could scientists ever really engineer a genome in the embryo to grow into this ideal child? Most experts agree that someday we will design genomes for physical features, such as hair and eye color and height. But they doubt that we could ever engineer talents and personality. There is no such thing as a math gene or a shyness gene, as far as scientists can tell. And talents and personality grow little by little, day by day. They don't just show up all at once. Still, some experts insist that designer babies of some kind will exist one day.

Human Cloning

All sorts of animals have been cloned by scientists: sheep, mice, cows, pigs, cats. But not humans. Not yet.

To clone a human, scientists would run through the same steps it took to clone Dolly the sheep (see page 26). They would put the nucleus from the parent's cell into an empty egg, put the egg into a woman, and wait for the egg to grow into a live human baby. Clones share the same genome, so parent and child would look a lot alike. But each one would still have his or her own special personality.

Scientists have tried creating human clones in a laboratory. So far no one has succeeded. But experts say that eventually a human likely will be cloned and more will follow.

Many people strongly oppose human cloning and designer babies. They believe creating life should be left to Mother Nature. Each child's

These identical triplets are human clones that occurred naturally.

genome should be new and unique, a never-before-seen combination of the parents' genomes, as nature intends.

Some scientists disagree. They say that parents already mold and shape their children in many different ways. They give them piano lessons and send them to computer and basketball camps. They give them advice on what to wear and eat and whom their friends should be. So why shouldn't parents be allowed to shape their children's genomes too? What do you think?

FUN FACT!

Have you ever met identical twins? Then you know human clones. Identical twins come from the same fertilized egg. So do identical triplets and quadruplets!

Glossary

adult stem cells: cells that can become any kind of tissue the body needs

bacteria: single-celled living organisms

cell: the basic unit of any living organism. Cells carry on the processes of life, according to instructions they get from genes.

chromosomes: rod-shaped structures in the nucleus of most cells that contain genes. Humans have twenty-three pairs of chromosomes.

clone: an exact copy of a gene, of a whole cell, or of a complete organism

designer babies: babies created through genetic engineering whose genes have been changed according to the parents' wishes

DNA (deoxyribonucleic acid): the molecule in the nucleus of most cells that holds genetic information passed from parent to child during reproduction

embryo: a developing creature in the very early stages of life

enzymes: proteins that makes reactions occur more quickly or efficiently

gene: a unit of chemicals in the genome that holds instructions for how to make one or more proteins

gene therapy: an experimental procedure to repair damaged genes or replace them with healthy genes

genetic engineering: changing genes to create new organisms

genome: all the genetic material in the chromosomes of an organism

knockout mouse: a mouse used in genetic engineering experiments. Scientists knock out, or disable, one or more genes to find out what instructions those genes carry.

mutation: a random, accidental change in an organism's DNA. Mutations can be harmless, harmful, or helpful.

nucleus: the central part of a cell that contains the genome

pharming: engineering plants or animals to make medicines

protein: a molecule created according to instructions from a gene. Proteins carry out all the processes of life, from making the hair on your head to breaking down food in your stomach.

selective breeding: breeding only the very best plants or animals to produce superior offspring

transgenic: having genes from more than one species. An organism is transgenic when one or more genes from another species have been engineered into its genome.

vaccine: a preparation of weakened viruses or bacteria that helps build up the body's defenses against diseases and that immunizes, or protects, an organism from disease

virus: a tiny organism that produces a disease by copying itself in another organism's cells

Selected Bibliography

Aldridge, Susan. *The Thread of Life: The Story of Genes and Genetic Engineering.* Cambridge, UK: Cambridge University Press, 1996.

Bryson, Bill. *A Short History of Nearly Everything.* New York: Broadway Books, 2003.

Hubbell, Sue. *Shrinking the Cat: Genetic Engineering before We Knew about Genes.* Boston: Houghton Mifflin, 2001.

Stock, Gregory. *Redesigning Humans: Our Inevitable Genetic Future.* Boston: Houghton Mifflin, 2002.

Further Reading and Websites

Balkwill, Fran. *DNA Is Here to Stay*. Minneapolis: Carolrhoda Books, Inc., 1993.

Cefrey, Holly. *Cloning and Genetic Engineering*. New York: Children's Press, 2002.

Fridell, Ron. *Decoding Life: Unraveling the Mysteries of the Genome*. Minneapolis: Lerner Publications Company, 2005.

Marshall, Elizabeth L. *High Tech Harvest*. Danbury, CT: Franklin Watts, 1999.

Nardo, Don. *Cloning*. San Diego: Lucent Books, 2002.

Seiple, Samantha, and Todd Seiple. *Mutants, Clones, and Killer Corn: Unlocking the Secrets of Biotechnology*. Minneapolis: Lerner Publications Company, 2005.

Snedden, Robert. *DNA & Genetic Engineering*. Chicago: Heinemann Library, 2003.

Torr, James D., ed. *Genetic Engineering: Opposing Viewpoints*. San Diego: Greenhaven Press, 2001.

DNA from the Beginning

http://www.dnaftb.org/dnaftb/

This comprehensive website uses text, images, and animation to explain the basics of genetics and genetic engineering.

Ethical, Legal, and Social Issues—Genome Research

http://www.ornl.gov/sci/techresources/Human_Genome/elsi/elsi.shtml

This section of the Human Genome Project's website discusses ethical issues. It includes articles about privacy, gene therapy, genetically modified foods, and also includes links to other websites.

Guardian Unlimited Picture Gallery

http://www.guardian.co.uk/gall/0,8542,627251,00.html

This website showcases photos and basic information about recently cloned animals.

Photo Acknowledgments

The images in this book are used with permission of: Mitch Doktycz, Life Sciences Division, Oak Ridge National Laboratory; U.S. Department of Energy Human Genome Program, <http://www.ornl.gov.hgmis>, background image throughout and p. 38; © Jim Richardson/CORBIS, p. 4 (left); © Rob C. Nunnington; Gallo Images/CORBIS, p. 4 (right); © Jeff Albertson/CORBIS, p. 5; © A. Barrington Brown/Photo Researchers, Inc., p. 6; © L. Clarke/CORBIS, p. 8; © AP | Wide World Photos, pp. 9 (top), 16, 21 (bottom); © Clouds Hill Imaging Ltd./CORBIS, p. 9 (bottom); © Maximilian Stock Ltd./Science Photo Library, p. 10 (bottom); © PhotoDisc Royalty-Free by Getty Images, pp. 10 (top), 40 (top); © Hulton Archive/Getty Images, p. 12 (top); © Sam Lund/Independent Picture Service, pp. 12 (bottom), 14; © Kent Foster/Visuals Unlimited, p. 13 (top); © Agricultural Research Service, USDA, p. 13 (bottom); © Douglas Peebles/CORBIS, p. 15 (left); © Lester V. Bergman/CORBIS, p. 15 (right); © Joel W. Rogers/CORBIS, p. 17; © Bojan Brecelj/CORBIS, p. 18; © Herbert Gehr/Time Life Pictures/Getty Images, p. 19; © Nikolas Konstantinou/Getty Images, p. 21 (top); © Sally A. Morgan; Ecoscene/CORBIS, p. 22; © University of Guelph, Ontario, Canada, p. 23; © Bruce Dale/National Geographic/Getty Images, p. 24; © www.glofish.com, p. 25 (upper left and right); © SAM YEH/AFP/Getty Images, p. 25 (upper center); © MC LEOD MURDO/CORBIS, p. 25 (lower right, all); © John Downer/Getty Images, p. 27 (top); © Brandon D. Cole/CORBIS, p. 27 (bottom); © Jim Zuckerman/CORBIS, p. 28; © Ted Thai/Time Life Pictures/Getty Images, p. 29; © SCF/Visuals Unlimited, p. 30 (top); © Peter Macdiarmid/Reuters/CORBIS, p. 30 (bottom); © David A. Northcott/CORBIS, p. 31; © David A. Wells/CORBIS, p. 32 (top); © Getty Images, p. 32 (bottom); © Royalty-Free/CORBIS, pp. 33, 34, 36; © Genetic Savings & Clone, p. 35; © Yann Arthus-Bertrand/CORBIS, p. 37; © Lester Lefkowitz/CORBIS, p. 39; © Johannes Eisele/AFP/Getty Images, p. 40 (bottom); © Paul Barton/CORBIS, p. 42.

Front cover: Mitch Doktycz, Life Sciences Division, Oak Ridge National Laboratory; U.S. Department of Energy Human Genome Program, <http://www.ornl.gov.hgmis>, (background image and right); © Comstock Images (left); www.glofish.com (center); © David A. Northcott/CORBIS, (mouse).

About the Author

Ron Fridell has written for radio, television, and newspapers. He has also written books about the Human Genome Project and the use of DNA to solve crimes. In addition to writing books, Mr. Fridell regularly visits libraries and schools to conduct workshops on nonfiction writing. He lives in Evanston, Illinois.

AUSTRALIA

ROBERT PROSSER

Evans

TITLES IN THE COUNTRIES OF THE WORLD SERIES:
ARGENTINA • AUSTRALIA • BRAZIL • CANADA • CHILE
CHINA • EGYPT • FRANCE • GERMANY • INDIA • INDONESIA
ITALY • JAPAN • KENYA • MEXICO • NIGERIA • POLAND
RUSSIA • SOUTH KOREA • SPAIN • SWEDEN • UNITED KINGDOM
USA • VIETNAM

Published by Evans Brothers Limited
2A Portman Mansions
Chiltern Street
London W1U 6NR

VISIT OUR WEBSITE
www.evansbooks.co.uk
Evans

Reprinted with revisions 2007

Produced for Evans Brothers Limited by
Monkey Puzzle Media Limited
Gissing's Farm, Fressingfield
Suffolk IP21 5SH, UK

British Library Cataloguing in Publication Data
Prosser, Robert
Australia. – (Countries of the world)
1.Australia – Juvenile literature
I. Title
994

ISBN 0 237 53286 7
13-digit ISBN (from 1 January 2007) 978 0 237 53286 4

Editor: Susie Brooks
Designer: Jane Hawkins
Map artwork by Peter Bull
Charts and graph artwork by Encompass Graphics Ltd

Picture acknowledgements
All photographs are by Bill Bachman, except *ANT Photo
Library* 15 (Gordon Claridge), 33 bottom (Bill Bachman), 52
top (Jack Cameron), 56 (Nick Tonks), 57 (Natural Images);
Corbis Digital Stock front and back endpapers; *Holden Ltd*
46; *Mike Langford* 43 top; *Port Waratah Coal Services,
Newcastle* 48 bottom; *Bill Sampson* 17 top right; *Wildlight
Photo Agency* 37 top (Philip Quirk).

Endpapers (front): Sydney Opera House and
business district, seen from across the harbour.
Title page: Mustering sheep in the Outback.
Imprint and Contents page: A farm on the
Stirling plains in Western Australia's wheat belt.
Endpapers (back): Uluru (Ayers Rock).

The Australian flag is made up of the Union Jack (top left), the Star of Federation (bottom left) and the stars of the Southern Cross constellation.

Australia is a land of glorious coastlines and other spectacular scenery.

Australia is the sixth-largest country in the world and the second-largest island (after Greenland). Because of its immense size and isolation, it is also considered a continent in itself. Australia lies in the Oceania region of the southern hemisphere, between the Indian and South Pacific Oceans. It consists of a vast main island, plus Tasmania – a small island state to the south-east – and several tiny coastal islands.

Compared to most countries, Australia has a short political history. European settlers claimed the land in 1788, and for more than 100 years it was divided into separate British colonies. It was not until 1901 that six of these colonies joined together as a federation of states (Queensland, New South Wales, Victoria, Tasmania, South Australia and Western Australia). In 1911, two final territories joined (Northern Territory and Canberra, Australian Capital Territory).

THE COMMONWEALTH

Each of Australia's states has its own parliament and its own identity, but the central, federal government is based in the nation's capital, Canberra. The federal system is known formally as the Commonwealth of Australia, and when Australians refer to 'the Commonwealth' they usually mean their own country and government. This can be confusing as Australia, having once been a colony, is still a member of the British Commonwealth. Although Australia is an independent country, the British queen is legally the Head of State, with a Governor General acting as her representative. It is likely that in the future this link with the UK will be broken and Australia will become a republic.

ABORIGINAL ORIGINS

Although British settlers did not arrive until the eighteenth century, Australia's cultural history extends much further back in time. The first inhabitants were the Aborigines, who migrated there from South-east Asia at least 50,000 years ago. In 1788 there were approximately 300,000 Aborigines, scattered across the country in semi-nomadic groups. Today many Aborigines remain, though their lifestyles have largely changed.

An aboriginal guide tells traditional stories at Uluru (Ayers Rock) in Northern Territory.

Balloons float over Canberra on Canberra Day, a yearly festival marking the city's birthday.

PACIFIC LINKS

Australia retains close ties with the UK, but its economic and political future lies increasingly across the Pacific world. This stretches from the USA to the expanding economies of East and South-east Asia. Australia has made a number of trade, military and security pacts within this broad region, often in partnership with its neighbour New Zealand.

KEY DATA

Area:	7,686,850km^2
Population:	20,583,000 (2006)
Capital City:	Canberra, Australian Capital Territory
Other Main Cities:	Sydney, Melbourne, Brisbane, Perth
Currency:	Australian Dollar (A$)
GDP Per Capita:	US$30,331*
Highest Point:	Mount Kosciusko (2,228m)

*(2004) Calculated on Purchasing Power Parity basis
Source: World Bank

Giant termite mounds in the Tanami Desert, Northern Territory.

Australia has a widely varied landscape, ranging from rocky uplands to flat lowland plains, and from barren deserts to tropical offshore reefs. On the whole it is an arid country, so green grasslands and lush forests are found only in limited areas.

THE LIE OF THE LAND

Australia's landmass has four distinctive features:

- Despite its huge size, it is a 'low' continent – the highest point is only 2,228m.
- It is an ancient and stable island with few recently-formed rocks. There is no present-day volcanic activity and fault movements are rare.
- There are vast expanses of relatively flat land. This is because erosion has worn down the landscape over many millions of years.
- Landforms change very slowly due to the generally dry climate. Vigorous carving of valleys and gorges is restricted to the moister eastern uplands and temperate Tasmania.

LANDSCAPE FEATURES

UPLANDS

Australia's upland areas are low compared to mountain ranges in most other countries. Nevertheless, they form impressive landscapes that vary physically from place to place.

THE GREAT DIVIDING RANGE

Australia's largest continuous upland range runs in an arc for 4,000km from the Cape York Peninsula to southern Victoria, following the east coast of the continent. It is known as the Great Dividing Range, though today it is not as massive as this name suggests because the rocks have been worn down by erosion. Even the most rugged regions, such as the Snowy Mountains in the south, are mostly below 2,000m. The highest peak is Mount Kosciusko, at 2,228m. In Queensland, few areas rise above 1,000m and there are broad plateaux and tablelands, separated by lines of hills.

The Great Dividing Range is asymmetrical. A steep edge faces the coast, while the inland slopes are gentler, sinking steadily to the Central Lowlands. Rivers have cut deeply into the eastern slopes, producing some stunning scenery such as Queensland's Mossman Gorge. Although Australia's east coast has many superb beaches, including Bondi and Fraser Island (the world's largest sand island), the coastal lowlands are generally narrow. In many districts, the hills slope directly to the sea.

INTERIOR RANGES

There are a number of hill ranges scattered across Australia. Examples are the Flinders Range in South Australia, the Macdonnell Ranges in Northern Territory, the Selwyn Range in Queensland and the Hammersley Range in Western Australia. Most are arranged in ridges or clusters, often separated by tablelands or valleys. They appear higher than they actually are because they rise suddenly from vast areas of flat land. Many are built of ancient rocks that contain valuable minerals including silver, copper, nickel, lead and zinc.

TASMANIA

During the last ice age, when sea levels were lower, Tasmania was joined to mainland Australia. Today it is separated by the water of the Bass Strait. Apart from a low coastal plain in the north, Tasmania is a mountainous island. Along the western side there are steep hills called the Tasmanian Ridges. Much of the centre and east of the island is made up of plateaux of resistant rocks, such as the Lakes Plateau. Between these blocks is a zone of lower land called the Midlands Plain, worn down from less resistant rocks.

Tasmania is the only part of Australia that was cold enough for vast icefields and glaciers to grow during the last ice age. The ice vigorously eroded the land, creating rugged terrain and numerous lakes. Lake St Clair, the deepest lake in Australia, lies in a cavernous glacial trough. Today, rain falls year-round on the western mountain ridges and fast-running streams continue to wear away the rocks.

The Macdonnell Ranges rise in rocky ridges near Glen Helen Gorge, west of Alice Springs.

LOWLANDS

Australia's huge north–south lowland zone can
be divided into three main regions, each based
on wide-ranging river drainage systems.

THE CARPENTARIA LOWLANDS

Fringing the Gulf of Carpentaria on the north coast
of the continent, the remote Carpentaria lowlands
are made up of gently sloping, poorly-drained plains
and tropical wetlands. The flat terrain is interrupted
occasionally by low sandstone plateaux.

THE GREAT ARTESIAN BASIN

The Great Artesian Basin – so named because of
the water-bearing rocks that underlie it (see page 33)
– measures approximately 1,600km from north to
south and 1,200km from east to west. The area
is covered by a network of non-permanent streams
that run south-west into Lake Eyre.

   The climate becomes increasingly dry towards the
west and the landscape reflects this change. In the
east and centre of the basin the main landforms are
wide, flat floodplains of sand, gravel and pebbles.
These are separated by low, flat-topped hills, mostly
sandstone. Across the western section of the region
there are huge desert landscapes. These include
sandy surfaces such as the Simpson Desert, north of
Lake Eyre, and flat, stony surfaces such as the Sturt
Stony Desert to the east. Lake Eyre itself is empty for
much of the time and you are most likely to see it
as broad sheets of silt and salt flats, known as playas.

THE MURRAY-DARLING BASIN

The drainage area of the River Murray and its
major tributaries – the River Darling and the River
Murrumbidgee – forms a broad lowland plain. The
rivers collect most of their water in the rainy uplands
of the Great Dividing Range and they have year-round
flows that vary from season to season. During heavy
rains there is regular flooding and expansive marshy
surfaces have formed. Sediment arriving at the
mouth of the River Murray near Adelaide has helped
to create sand dunes and offshore sand bars along
the south-east coast of South Australia.

The sandy plains of the Simpson Desert remain largely
arid, except for brief spells after irregular winter rains.

PLAINS AND PLATEAUX

For some 3.5 million km^2 across the arid western half of Australia, wide open landscape is typical. If you drive across in a four-wheel-drive vehicle (essential due to lack of surfaced roads) you will experience long, monotonous hours when nothing seems to change. But occasionally you'll see sudden contrasts that interrupt the flatness, such as a set of steep, red-rock hills or a white, dried-up lakebed shimmering in the heat. Subtle variations crop up too, though you may not notice them at first.

If you take a much broader view, say from an aircraft, it is possible to group this environment into three landscape types: sandy surfaces, stony surfaces, and broad areas of bare, solid rock. The most common of these, covering 1 million km^2, is sand – either sand plains or sand dunes. The dunes can be arc-shaped, but they mostly run in straight lines. In these massive linear dunefields, individual dunes may stretch for 20km and the crests of two parallel dunes may be 1km apart. Over most of Australia's interior, the sand surfaces are held in place by patchy vegetation or hard surface crusts, so moving dunes are rare.

Uluru (Ayers Rock) rises abruptly from a vast area of flat land in the dry 'Red Heart' of the continent.

AN EXTREME CLIMATE

One of the outstanding features of Australia is its dryness. Moister climates are limited to the fringes and the eastern uplands, and rainfall totals decrease rapidly inland. At least one-third of the country has on average less than 250mm annual rainfall, though patterns are unpredictable and totals can vary greatly from year to year. Much of Australia is also consistently hot due to long hours of strong sunshine. This means that an unusually high proportion of rainwater is lost through evaporation.

CLIMATE ZONES

TEMPERATURE AND RAINFALL

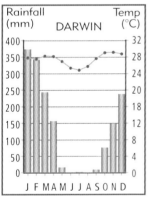

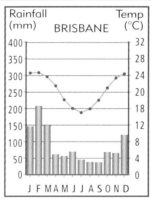

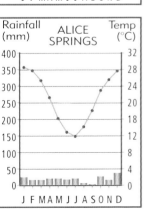

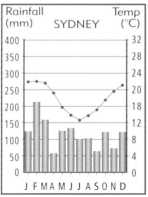

CLIMATIC REGIONS

The map above divides Australia into five generalised climatic regions, based on patterns of rainfall and average temperatures. Each region covers a huge area, so there will be local variation within each one.

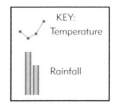

KEY:
Temperature

Rainfall

TROPICAL AND SUB-TROPICAL NORTH AND NORTH-EAST

In north and north-eastern Australia, the climate is ruled by the seasonal movement of the tropical monsoon. During the Australian summer (November–March) warm, moist monsoon air sweeps across the north and north-east coasts. Rains come in regular, heavy deluges and can deposit more than 1,600mm a year over the mountains. During the winter the monsoon belt moves northwards and is replaced by hot, dry air that drifts across from inland areas where far less rain falls.

Summer temperatures in the far northern tropics average well over 20°C, and the weather feels hot and 'sticky' due to very high humidities. Winters remain hot with little cloud, and only along the coasts do sea breezes bring relief. People wait anxiously for the first rains to break the heat, which regularly sizzles over 30°C. Yet when the rains do arrive, the humid air makes life exhausting. Moving southwards down the east Queensland coast, the climate becomes sub-tropical and levels of heat and moisture, though high, become less extreme.

CASE STUDY
TROPICAL CYCLONES IN BABINDA, QUEENSLAND

Babinda is a small town on the coast of tropical Queensland. During the summer monsoon season, more than 250mm of rain may fall in one day. In most years at least one tropical cyclone hits the coast and the intensity of wind and rain can be amazing. On one occasion, more than 350mm of rain was recorded to have fallen in a space of seven hours. At the height of this deluge, more than 10mm of rain blasted the town within a five-minute period. During a cyclone, sheets of muddy water pour from nearby agricultural slopes and flood the town. Local people are left to clear the sticky red mud from the streets and fill in deep gullies eroded on the farmland.

Heavy seasonal rain blasts the vegetation of a tropical rainforest in north-east Queensland.

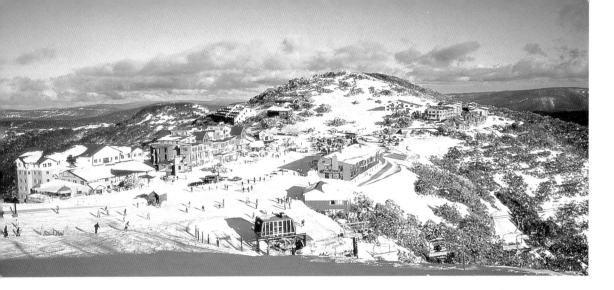

TEMPERATE SOUTH-EAST AND SOUTH-WEST AUSTRALIA

Down the coast from Brisbane, temperatures become more moderate and the seasonal pattern of rainfall changes. In an arc that includes Melbourne, Adelaide and part of the River Murray Basin, most rain comes in winter. For example, in a normal year, 60 per cent of Adelaide's rain falls between May and August.

This seasonal bias is caused by the west–east movement of mid-latitude depressions. These are areas of low pressure that, in winter, bring cloud, rain and some snow to south-west and south-east Australia. In summer they normally pass further south and so bring less rain to the mainland.

The name Snowy Mountains tells us that high areas have regular snow – in some cases enough to support ski resorts. But in non-mountainous areas, temperatures in this zone remain mild in the winter (10–15°C) and rise rapidly during the summer. The summer average is 20–28°C, though there are frequent hotter spells. During the Australian Open Tennis Championship in Melbourne in January 2003, daytime temperatures reached a scorching 34°C. When these heatwaves occur during drought years, there is a high risk of serious bush fires.

The south-west corner of Australia, centred on Perth, enjoys a form of Mediterranean climate, with well-defined mild, damp winters and hot, dry summers. Rainfall totals drop and average temperatures rise rapidly as you move further inland.

ABOVE: Mount Hotham Alpine Resort attracts skiers to the mountains of north-east Victoria.
RIGHT: Hot sun dries and cracks the mud on the northern shore of Lake Eyre in South Australia.

THE ARID/SEMI-ARID INTERIOR

The average rainfall across Australia's huge interior is less than 250mm a year. However, average figures are not always useful because what stands out here is the unreliability of the rainfall. Cattle ranchers in the hot, dry plains know that 400mm of rain one year may be followed by 100mm, or less, the next.

Australia has no extreme deserts and even the driest areas receive some rain. It comes as occasional heavy downpours when monsoon storms stray south from the tropics, or when depressions shift unusually far north. As these moist air masses move inland the air is heated by the hot land surface. Strong convection currents can then cause severe thunderstorms.

In the arid/semi-arid region there are few clouds and days are extended with long hours of sunshine. For at least six months of the year, daytime temperatures may exceed 30°C. At night, the skies are cool and a diurnal range (difference in temperature between day and night) of 20°C is not unusual.

This can be an extremely harsh climate – a difficult one in which to live. Months of dry heat may be broken by heavy rainstorms and sudden flash floods. Then, when the skies clear, any water that does not seep into the ground quickly evaporates and within days the hot, cloudless weather returns.

Bush fires are a real threat in the dry summer heat of much of central and southern Australia.

TEMPERATE TASMANIA

Tasmania lies far enough south to be in the path of the mid-latitude depressions all year round. These depressions have crossed the vast southern oceans and can bring strong winds and continuously cloudy weather. Rain falls in every season, usually with a winter maximum. Except for the south-east corner, Tasmania receives an average rainfall of at least 1,000mm per year. Compared with the rest of Australia, the rain is generally reliable and rivers therefore run year-round. Australians are very fond of 'Tasie' because its moderate, mixed climate and cool running streams are so different from the severe extremes of so much of their country.

Tasmania's temperate environment encourages outdoor leisure activities such as fly-fishing.

A UNIQUE ECOLOGY

Australia has a very distinctive collection of plants and animals, many unique to the continent. For example, there are marsupials such as kangaroos, wallabies, wombats and bandicoots, which carry their young in pouches. One of the joys of walking or camping – especially in the wetter regions – is hearing the songs of a wonderful variety of birds, such as the piercing laugh of the kookaburra. There are giant tree ferns and a wide range of eucalyptus or 'gum' trees, from massive red gums to tall, thin stringybarks with their long strips of hanging grey bark.

VEGETATION REGIONS

Australia can be broadly split into differing vegetation regions, as seen on the map below. In most places the change from one region to another is gradual. Vegetation type is closely related to water availability, temperature and how the plants adapt to the conditions – lush rainforests bloom in tropical monsoon areas, for example, while cacti and bunch grasses survive desert droughts. Many types of eucalyptus and acacia trees grow in surprisingly dry areas, though the less water there is, the smaller and sparser they become.

A baby kangaroo, or 'joey', will not leave its mother's pouch until it is able to fend for itself.

VEGETATION AND SURFACE TYPES

Sand plains and dunes

Stony plains

Broad rock surfaces

Tropical monsoon woodland and rainforest

Temperate woodland and forest

Dry savannah with short grasses, scrub and scattered trees

Drought-resistant open woodland and scrub

Sparse desert vegetation

0   500   1000km
0   600 miles

Gulf of Carpentaria

Great Barrier Reef

N

Tropic of Capricorn

Lake Eyre

Great Australian Bight

SOUTHERN OCEAN

Tasman Sea

TASMANIA

LEFT: Eucalyptus trees, such as these in the Karri Forest, Western Australia, can grow to over 60m.

RIGHT: The kookaburra – a type of king-fisher – is unique to the Australian continent.

EFFECTS OF ISOLATION

Australia's unusual species have evolved because the island has been isolated from other landmasses for many millions of years. This has allowed the plants and animals to adapt well to local conditions. For example, kangaroos and wallabies have developed strong rear legs and bounding movements to help them travel long distances in search of food and water. They can also stretch upwards to reach leaves from shrubs and trees. Koala, in aboriginal language, means 'I don't drink', because eucalyptus leaves – the only things koalas eat – provide all the moisture they need.

Another important legacy of Australia's isolation is that native animals and birds have evolved as part of a distinct ecosystem. They have developed survival techniques based on local predator-prey relationships – but they are highly vulnerable when new species are introduced from abroad. Many such species have been introduced since European settlers arrived in 1788. Because they come from different ecosystems and have no natural predators in Australia, most have thrived. Animals such as cattle, sheep, foxes, dogs, cats, rats and mice compete with native species for food. The best-known intruder is the rabbit. Today its population is counted in the hundreds of millions and it has become a national plague (see page 52).

EXAMPLES OF AUSTRALIA'S ECOLOGICAL DIVERSITY

Eucalypts ('gum trees')	More than 500 species
Acacias ('wattles')	More than 600 species
Marsupials	More than 120 species
Snakes	160 species, of which two-thirds are venomous
Parrots	50 species
Cockatoos	11 species, out of only 12 in the world
Dingos	Claimed to be the world's oldest wild dog species
Fish	More than 2,000 species, including 90 species of sharks

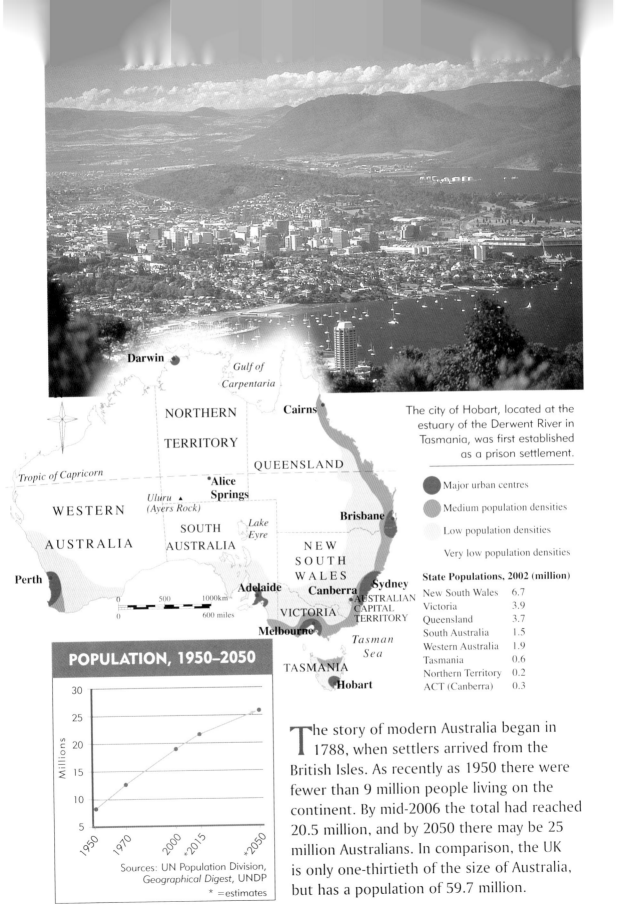

Darwin

Gulf of
Carpentaria

NORTHERN

TERRITORY

Cairns

Tropic of Capricorn

•**Alice
Springs**

Uluru ▲
(Ayers Rock)

QUEENSLAND

WESTERN

AUSTRALIA

SOUTH
AUSTRALIA

*Lake
Eyre*

Brisbane

NEW
SOUTH
WALES

Perth

Adelaide

Canberra•

Sydney

0   500   1000km

0   600 miles

VICTORIA

AUSTRALIAN
CAPITAL
TERRITORY

Melbourne

*Tasman
Sea*

TASMANIA

Hobart

The city of Hobart, located at the
estuary of the Derwent River in
Tasmania, was first established
as a prison settlement.

⬤ Major urban centres

⬤ Medium population densities

Low population densities

Very low population densities

State Populations, 2002 (million)

New South Wales	6.7
Victoria	3.9
Queensland	3.7
South Australia	1.5
Western Australia	1.9
Tasmania	0.6
Northern Territory	0.2
ACT (Canberra)	0.3

POPULATION, 1950–2050

Millions

30

25

20

15

10

5

1950   1970   2000 *2015   *2050

Sources: UN Population Division,
Geographical Digest, UNDP

* =estimates

The story of modern Australia began in
1788, when settlers arrived from the
British Isles. As recently as 1950 there were
fewer than 9 million people living on the
continent. By mid-2006 the total had reached
20.5 million, and by 2050 there may be 25
million Australians. In comparison, the UK
is only one-thirtieth of the size of Australia,
but has a population of 59.7 million.

POPULATION CLUSTERS

The Australian population is very unevenly distributed. Eight out of ten people live on only 2 per cent of the land and within 80km of the coast. At the other extreme, barely 500,000 people are scattered across 80 per cent of the continent. Two out of three Australians live in or near the six state capitals.

SETTLEMENT PATTERNS

Before the federation of states was established, Australia was divided into separate British colonies, each with its own capital. Several, such as Hobart and Brisbane, began as prison settlements. Until well into the nineteenth century, convicts from the UK were transported to prisons in Australia. Many stayed on as settlers when they were released.

Immigrants in colonial times arrived by ship, so ports such as Sydney and Perth became the main towns. As the economy grew, farming and mineral products were exported through these ports. New settlements and transport routes spread slowly inland, but populations clustered mainly around the coasts. During the 1990s, two-thirds of Australia's population growth was focussed on four major centres – Sydney, Melbourne, Perth and Brisbane. The most rapid growth occurs at the edges of urban areas and in attractive coastal and mountain regions.

POPULATION GROWTH

At present, Australia's population is growing by about 1.1 per cent a year. This growth is explained by two components: natural change (the difference between numbers of births and deaths, usually expressed as a rate per 1,000 population) and migration (the movement of people in and out of the country). The table (above right) shows how this worked in 2002, when Australia's population grew by 252,000.

NATURAL CHANGE

As in most countries, Australia's birth rates are falling. In 1995, there were 14.2 births per 1,000 population. By 2004 this had dropped to 12.7. Meanwhile, mortality (death) rates have stayed at around 6.6 per 1,000 people. So the number of births still exceeds the number of deaths, creating a natural increase.

But to sustain a population over time, fertility rates need to be at least two live births per woman. Australia's average is less than this. So, although deaths among infants are decreasing (see graph below), there are still too few people in the younger age groups. This means that immigration will become increasingly important if Australia's population is to continue to grow.

POPULATION CHANGE DURING 2002

NATURAL CHANGE

Births	247,000
Deaths	133,000
Natural increase	114,000

MIGRATION

Immigrants	358,000
Emigrants	220,000
Net migration	138,000

TOTAL CHANGE
114,000 + 138,000 = 252,000

Source: Australian Government Website

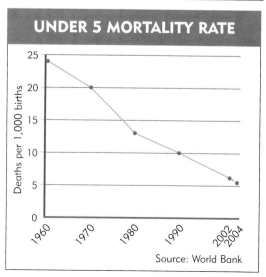

UNDER 5 MORTALITY RATE

Source: World Bank

ORIGIN OF IMMIGRANT RESIDENTS IN AUSTRALIA, 2001

COUNTRY	NUMBER
UK	1,210,000
New Zealand	375,000
Italy	242,000
Former Yugoslavia	210,100
Vietnam	175,000
China	168,000
Greece	141,000
Philippines	123,000

Source: Australian Government Website

Melbourne's thriving Chinatown is evidence of the city's substantial immigrant population.

MIGRATION

Migration is the movement of people to and from a given place. The difference between numbers of immigrants (those who come in) and emigrants (those who leave) is known as the net migration balance. In Australia, there have generally been more immigrants than emigrants, and this has been important to population growth.

In the mid-twentieth century, immigration was based on a 'White Australia' policy. The government was worried that Australia's

CASE STUDY
THE PIAZZA FAMILY FROM ITALY

Ron Piazza lives in a Brisbane suburb and has a job at a civil engineering company. His father migrated from Italy during the 1950s and worked on sugar farms and banana plantations in northern Queensland. Italians were popular employees because they were willing to work in the hot climate. Ron's father lived in a small town near Cairns, where he met and married a girl from Italy. He worked on sugar farms for 20 years, and they had three children – Ron,

Maria and Joe. By 1980 sugar production was becoming more mechanised and Ron's parents were getting older. So the family moved to an Italian neighbourhood in Brisbane. The parents ran a bakery and pasta shop until they retired. They now live in a small retirement community on the Queensland coast.

Ron and his brother and sister have all visited Italy but they speak little Italian. They all graduated from Australian universities. Maria and her Lebanese husband run a travel agency in Darwin, and Joe is a supermarket manager in Melbourne.

relatively small population would be overwhelmed by migrants from Asia's rapidly growing populations. By 1970 this policy was abandoned and Australia today is a multicultural society. In 2001, 4.5 million people in Australia were foreign-born.

THE REFUGEE PROBLEM

Australia is an attractive country both for voluntary migrants and for refugees fleeing their countries. This has caused strong

Foreign immigrants in Australia may take language classes to assist their integration.

arguments about the growing numbers of asylum seekers. There have been several waves of illegal immigrants into Australia. In 2001 the Australian Navy stopped boatloads of Afghan refugees from landing in Northern Territory.

POPULATION STRUCTURE

Australia has a 'mature' population structure – most people are in the family-raising age range of 20–50 years. High quality healthcare means low infant mortality rates – but fewer babies are now being born, life expectancies are rising and so the population is ageing. It is likely that by 2015 at least 15 per cent of the population will be over 65. The figure will be higher if immigration decreases because migrants are often young people with large families.

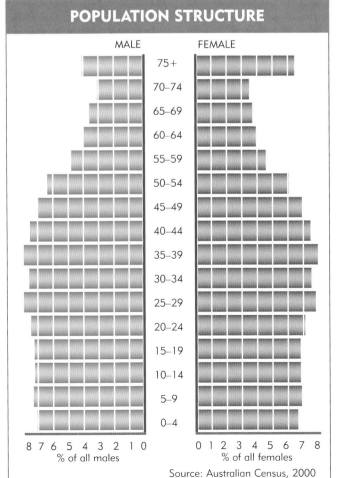

POPULATION STRUCTURE

MALE   FEMALE

75+
70–74
65–69
60–64
55–59
50–54
45–49
40–44
35–39
30–34
25–29
20–24
15–19
10–14
5–9
0–4

8 7 6 5 4 3 2 1 0   0 1 2 3 4 5 6 7 8
% of all males   % of all females

Source: Australian Census, 2000

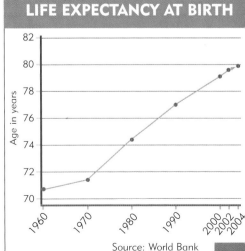

LIFE EXPECTANCY AT BIRTH

Source: World Bank

THE ABORIGINAL POPULATION

There were probably 300,000 Aborigines spread throughout Australia in 1788. But the 1981 Census recorded barely 200,000 people as Aborigines. In the 2001 Census, however, numbers had risen again to 458,500. This is because people of mixed descent as well as full-blood Aborigines are now counted as 'aboriginal'. The aboriginal story falls into three broad chapters, as follows.

PRE-EUROPEAN: UP TO 1788

Aborigines have lived in Australia for at least 50,000 years. They were originally semi-nomadic people who circulated in small tribal groups, or 'bands'. They moved over terratorial 'homelands' to find food and water, and developed a close relationship with the environment. According to tradition, the homeland belonged to the tribal group (not to individuals) forever, and it had deep religious meaning.

EXCLUSION AND OPPRESSION: 1788–1950

European settlement brought disaster to the Aborigines:

- They were pushed off their lands and denied legal rights. Many bands were crowded on to government reservations or Christian missions. Some stayed as stockmen or farmworkers.
- Government and missionary policies discouraged or banned traditional ways of life and even languages.
- Aboriginal peoples had no resistance to diseases such as smallpox and measles, introduced by Europeans.
- Europeans misunderstood Australian conditions. They overused the land, killed wildlife and sapped water supplies. They degraded the environmental resources on which Aborigines depended.

An aboriginal guide leads tourists on the 'Liru Walk' through groves of flowering mulla mulla plants near Uluru (Ayers Rock).

FORCES FOR REVIVAL

Aboriginals and 'aboriginal pride' movements today campaign for:

- Full citizenship and the right to vote.
- Improved housing, health and education conditions, leading to better job opportunities.
- Legal rights to traditional homelands.
- Reduction of prejudice and increased respect for aboriginal cultures.

THE STRUGGLE FOR REVIVAL: SINCE 1950

Aboriginal organisations have recently been working hard to revive their traditional culture, fighting especially for legal land rights and aboriginal pride. Strong efforts are also being made by the Australian government and citizens to correct the wrongs done to the aboriginal people.

The aboriginal population is growing once more, but Aborigines are still the poorest group in Australian society. Increasing numbers are moving to urban areas – most of New South Wales's 135,000 Aborigines live in and around Sydney. Only one in three Aborigines now remain in rural districts – the majority of these are found in remote parts

The Aboriginal Art and Culture Centre in Alice Springs promotes traditional tribal customs. It is owned and run by a local aboriginal group.

of Northern Territory and Western Australia, where some traditional ways of life may be maintained. As legal land rights are extended, aboriginal pride grows and more jobs become available, more aboriginal people are moving back to their original homelands.

CASE STUDY
THE NORTHERN LAND COUNCIL

Unfortunately tensions remain between aboriginal and European interests. Across vast areas of Australia's dry interior, ranchers rent grazing land from the government. They have campaigned to 'extinguish' all remaining aboriginal land rights. Aboriginal bodies fight for the reverse position – for permanent

rights to the homelands – and they have won several important legal battles in recent years. The Northern Land Council (NLC) is one such organisation. It was set up in 1973 to support traditional aboriginal landowners and other aboriginal people in Arnhem Land, Northern Territory. The NLC has regained legal title to its homelands and now leases one section to a uranium mining corporation and another large expanse to the government as the Kakadu National Park. These bring in money and jobs.

An older commercial street in Adelaide that has benefited from refurbishment.

Nine out of ten Australians today live in urban areas. These include great cities, suburban settlements, resorts, retirement communities and market and service towns scattered across the continent. The state capitals accommodate at least 50 per cent of the population. With the exception of Canberra, Australian Capital Territory, the capitals are all sited on natural harbours and act as major ports.

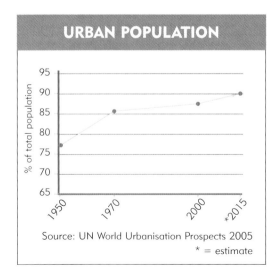

URBAN POPULATION

% of total population

95
90
85
80
75
70
65

1950   1970   2000   *2015

Source: UN World Urbanisation Prospects 2005
* = estimate

AUSTRALIAN CAPITAL TERRITORY

When Australia was united into a single nation in 1901, the city of Canberra was planned. It was built in the mountains of New South Wales and was given its own 'territory', or state. Canberra is the only major Australian city not on the coast. Today it is the seat of the Commonwealth government, with the formal title of Canberra, Australian Capital Territory (ACT). Despite its beautiful mountain setting, its inland position has not been able to compete with Sydney or Melbourne in attracting businesses or industries.

RECENT TRENDS

During the 1990s, 70 per cent of Australia's total population growth (equal to 830,000 people) occurred in and around Sydney, Melbourne, Perth and Brisbane. Australia's population is becoming increasingly concentrated in this way. For example, the Queensland coastal strip from Brisbane south to the New South Wales border is known as the Gold Coast. In 1970 it was a string of small beachside resorts. Today it is a 100km built-up strip of commuter, retirement and resort cities such as Surfers Paradise. Between 1991 and 2001, the total Gold Coast population exploded from 226,000 to a staggering 400,000.

The most rapid growth is in the outer towns. For example, the spread of Melbourne south-west around Port Phillip Bay has reached Geelong (see page 30). People and businesses move out from the older central cities. They are replaced by migrants from other regions of Australia and from abroad. Young people and recent immigrants are most likely to live in central cities. Families and older people move outwards to the suburbs and smaller towns.

In recent years the cities' Central Business Districts (CBDs) have grown, creating more jobs. Office space in downtown Perth doubled during the 1990s. Older, inner districts have been improved, or 'gentrified', attracting wealthier people and fashionable businesses including cafés and boutiques.

ABOVE: Surfers Paradise is just one of the ever-expanding resorts on the east Queensland coast.

RIGHT: Towering modern office blocks dominate the Perth skyline.

SMALL-TOWN AUSTRALIA

Meanwhile, many rural towns in Australia are suffering serious decline. Agriculture is changing and recently has been less prosperous, farmers and other rural people are increasingly mobile, and in many districts there are few jobs or career opportunities. Many smaller market towns are losing their function. Between 1990 and 2000, 50 per cent of towns with fewer than 5,000 people declined (see page 40).

Two types of town are avoiding these problems. Firstly, there are those within commuting distance of big cities or with accessible locations along main transport routes – towns up to 50km around Adelaide and along the Sydney–Melbourne road corridor, for example. This is part of a counterurbanisation process where people and businesses move from cities to smaller urban settlements for lower costs, improved standards of living and better working environments. Secondly, there are towns that are attractive to tourists and for retirement. Examples of these are found along the coastal zone between Brisbane and Rockhampton (Queensland) and north of Perth (Western Australia).

CASE STUDY: Sydney (Population, 2004: 4,254,900)

Sydney Harbour, with the Opera House left of the CBD, and the Harbour Bridge to the right.

Sydney is the capital of New South Wales and Australia's largest city. It is situated around a magnificent harbour, which is actually the estuary of the River Parramatta. The original settlement along the south side of the estuary is the site of the modern CBD, which boasts two of the world's best-known structures – the Sydney Harbour Bridge and the Opera House.

Modern Sydney covers the harbour basin, runs inland along the Parramatta valley and spills across the surrounding hills. As in all Australian cities, away from the centre the suburbs consist mainly of well-spaced one- and two-storey homes. Most affluent districts are in the hills north of the harbour. In 2004 to 2005, Sydney's population growth rate was 0.7 per cent, equivalent to 29,800 people a year. By 2021 there are likely to be 5 million inhabitants, with a demand for 500,000 extra homes. There is concern over the environmental impact of continued expansion. Lifestyles are water-oriented, based around the wonderful beaches and bays – the resort of Manly at the north entrance of the harbour, for example, is a popular commuter town.

Sydney lies at the centre of an urbanised region that runs 180km along the New South Wales coast from the coal and industrial port of Newcastle (population 300,000) to industrial Greater Wollongong (population 250,000). This is the most prosperous region of Australia. Sydney itself has 20 per cent of the country's population but 25 per cent of the income. Sydney is the main gateway for people, trade and finance. The prosperity is based on the so-called 'new economy', moving away from manufacturing to business, finance and information services. During the 1990s, 50,000 new jobs were created in the city, mostly in high-skilled business, science and technology

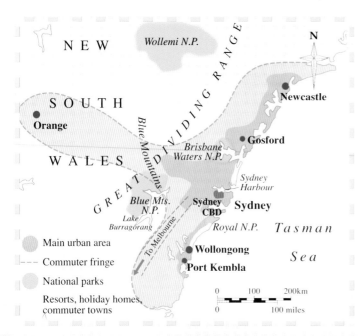

Main urban area

--- Commuter fringe

National parks

Resorts, holiday homes, commuter towns

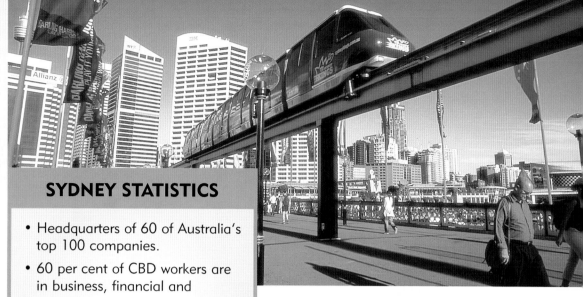

SYDNEY STATISTICS

- Headquarters of 60 of Australia's top 100 companies.
- 60 per cent of CBD workers are in business, financial and property services.
- Jobs in law and accounting professions increased by 60 per cent in the 1990s.
- One in two government jobs for the metropolitan region are in the city's CBD.
- 55 per cent of all international visitors to Australia pass through Sydney Airport.
- In 2004, more than 2.4 million visitors stayed in the city.

A monorail and pedestrian bridge make Sydney's CBD highly accessible to commuters.

professions. Sydney has overtaken Melbourne as Australia's business and finance capital. In 2001, 250 global corporations had their Australian headquarters in Sydney, compared with just 83 in Melbourne. Sydney has truly become a 'global city', especially since it staged the 2000 Olympic Games.

Cockle Bay Wharf on Darling Harbour is just one of Sydney's popular recreation areas.

Each year Sydney attracts 40 per cent of all immigrants to Australia. In the district of Erskineville, one in two schoolchildren are from ethnic minority groups and there is a successful Chinatown on the edge of the CBD. Many immigrants from Hong Kong, Singapore and Malaysia are professionals who have settled in the wealthier suburbs of north Sydney. Poorer, less skilled immigrants, often from Vietnam, Indonesia and China, live in older, inner suburbs in south Sydney.

As in all modern cities, increasing numbers of families have moved out to the suburbs and 50 per cent of Sydney's workforce now commutes. The inner districts are refilled with newcomers, such as immigrants and young Australians. Regeneration projects have led to the gentrification of some older areas as increasing numbers of professionals move in. These include disused industrial buildings along the River Parramatta, and The Rocks, a fashionable district by the bayfront.

Located beside the Yarra River, Melbourne is a dynamic city that competes with Sydney in terms of business, leisure and transport facilities.

Melbourne is the capital of Victoria, Australia's second-largest city and one of the country's earliest settlements. The original town was built by the mouth of the Yarra River, at the head of Port Phillip Bay where the CBD stands today – and the commercial port grew up nearby at Port Melbourne. The huge bay is a fine harbour and gives shelter from the storms that sweep through the Bass Strait.

Modern Melbourne and its sprawling suburbs extend around the bay and across the coastal floodplain, especially to the east. There are superb beaches, landscaped parks, golf courses where kangaroos graze, and top-class stadiums, including the Melbourne Cricket Ground. The spacious suburbs are comfortably shaded by trees. One of the city's attractive features is its public transport system. There is an efficient, cheap network of rail, light rail, tram and bus routes.

Melbourne people, like most Australians, enjoy relaxing outdoors, and a string of beachfront towns and marinas stretches south-east as far as Phillip Island. This island, about the size of the Isle of Wight, is an easy day-trip for locals, and a popular holiday destination. Attractions include beaches where fairy penguins can be seen each day, and the island has the circuit for the Australian car and motorcycle grand prix races.

In 2004 to 2005, Melbourne's population increased by 1.1 per cent, equivalent to 41,300 people. The rest of Victoria grew much more slowly. One-third of Melbourne's growth came from immigration, and in 2001 more than one in five residents were born outside Australia. There are

Map legend:

VICTORIA

To Sydney

Ballarat

Melbourne
Melbourne CBD

Brisbane Ranges N.P.

Geelong

Port Phillip Bay

N

Otway N.P.

Phillip Island

Ferry links with Tasmania

Wilson's Promontory N.P.

0   50   100km
0   50 miles

B a s s   S t r a i t

- Main urban area
- Commuter fringe
- National parks
- Resorts, holiday homes, commuter towns

Crowds gather by the water at Victoria Harbour in Melbourne's redeveloped docklands.

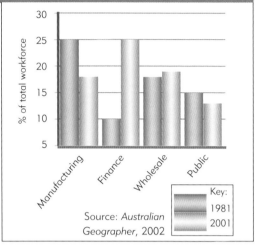

MELBOURNE'S MAIN ECONOMIC SECTORS

% of total workforce

Source: *Australian Geographer*, 2002

Key:
1981
2001

communities of Greeks, Italians and Lebanese who arrived in large numbers, especially during the 1970s and 1980s. More people of Greek origin live in Melbourne than in any other city outside Greece itself. More recently the main flows have been from South-east Asia and the Pacific islands. Many young people from Tasmania are also attracted to the city because of the direct ferry routes.

Melbourne generates 18 per cent of Australia's GDP. More than 80 multinational corporations have their Australian head offices in the fast-growing CBD. Greater Melbourne is more industrial than Sydney, despite a recent decline in manufacturing industries such as textiles and motor vehicles. Engineering businesses, petro-chemical complexes and the modern port facilities are mainly located to the west of the city, as far as Geelong.

As in Sydney, Melbourne's older inner districts are being regenerated. Derelict docks have been redeveloped for residential and leisure uses – for example, there is a very large casino along the riverfront close to the CBD, developed in part to attract tourists away from Sydney. Parts of old Port Melbourne have been gentrified – disused warehouses and other commercial buildings have become fashionable apartments, workshops and studios, and parks and cycle-ways weave through the district. Part of the attraction is the long beach and the light rail route that takes commuters and shoppers to the CBD in just 15 minutes. The main ferry terminal for Tasmania is Port Melbourne's only link with its maritime past.

Sydney and Melbourne are rivals. However, a survey in 2001 concluded that they are equal but different. Melbourne is well-placed to be the leading port and its capacity to move goods is far superior to that of Sydney. It is well located too, for what manufacturing remains in Australia. Sydney is primarily a financial and producer services centre. Easy transportation and communication between the two cities means that they can both benefit from each other's strengths.

Melbourne's light rail system is one of Australia's most efficient transport services.

AGRICULTURAL AND RURAL AUSTRALIA

Cattle grazing on the rolling pastures around Merrijig, north-east Victoria.

Outside the big cities, Australia becomes a vast rural country, sparsely scattered with small communities and isolated farmsteads. Farmlands range from intensive crop plantations to remote, dry expanses where only hardy cattle find grazing. There is a sense of space and emptiness about much of rural Australia.

WATER – THE VITAL RESOURCE

As we've seen, Australia is a dry continent – three-quarters of the country receives on average less than 500mm of rain a year and in many regions the rainfall is highly seasonal and unreliable. As a result, water availability is the crucial control on agriculture.

RIVER NETWORKS

The country's lack of rainfall is reflected in its river systems. Permanent streams that give year-round surface water are limited to the moister fringes and Tasmania. Elsewhere, streams are either seasonal – flowing during the wetter months – or ephemeral – flowing briefly after occasional storms.

DAMS AND RESERVOIRS

In relatively rainy areas, water can be stored behind dams in reservoirs. These supply water to farms and settlements downstream. Larger schemes, such as the Tinaroo Falls Dam in Queensland, often include hydroelectric power generation (HEP). One problem is loss of water through evaporation – the huge Lake Eildon reservoir in the headwaters of the River Murray (Victoria) is generally less than half full, partly because the Sun's powerful heat evaporates the water.

RIVER TO RIVER

Basin transfer is the transfer of water from one river basin with a surplus to another where demand exceeds supply. This involves costly engineering schemes but it is a useful way of distributing water. The largest and most famous system is the Snowy Mountains Project in New South Wales, built in the 1960s. Tunnels cut through the Great Dividing Range transfer water from rivers running coastwards, to headwater streams of the Murray Basin. HEP generators supply power to Canberra and the Sydney region.

ABOVE: Lake Kununurra and its dam store and divert water from the Ord River in Kimberley, Western Australia.

RIGHT: HEP generation at the Murray Power Station, part of the Snowy Mountains Project, New South Wales.

UNDERGROUND RESERVES

An alternative source of water is found, in some regions, beneath the surface. This groundwater is stored in aquifers – layers of rock that can retain water. The water arrives as rain in mountain areas, sinks into the ground and moves slowly through the aquifers. The largest of these groundwater stores is the Great Artesian Basin of New South Wales and Queensland. Wells have been drilled into the aquifers to allow agriculture to extend further into arid inland areas.

WATER AVAILABILITY REGIONS

We can divide Australia into four broad regions according to the main features of their water availability:

- Regions with sufficient surface and near-surface water to support plant growth through much of the year – for example Tasmania and the Great Dividing Range.
- Less moist regions with permanent stream networks to sustain water tables and supply irrigation systems – for example the River Murray Basin.
- Semi-arid regions with artesian groundwater that can be pumped out for irrigation and animals – for example the Great Artesian Basin in Queensland.
- Arid regions with ephemeral streams and few groundwater resources – for example much of the interior, sometimes known as the 'Red Heart', of the continent.

CHANGING IMPORTANCE

In 1900, agriculture produced 23 per cent of Australia's GDP, but by 2003 this had plummeted to 3.4 per cent. In 1970, 45 per cent of the country's export value came from agricultural products, but this had more than halved by 2001. In 2003 4.0 per cent of Australians were employed in agriculture, yet it is still a major industry. Four products lead the export rankings – meat, wool, grains, and grapes for wine. Cattle numbers are on the increase, cereal output is rising and arable land continues to expand.

AGRICULTURAL REGIONS

Australia's agricultural regions are dominated by two features. Firstly, cropland generally decreases and grazing increases as you move further inland. Secondly, the drier the environment, the less intensive the farming.

AUSTRALIA'S LEADING AGRICULTURAL EXPORTS, 2001

	OUTPUT (tonnes)	VALUE (A$ billion)	WORLD RANKING
Meat and animals	1.5 million	5.0	5th
Wheat and flour	15.8 million	3.2	2nd
Wool and wool yarn	465,000	2.2	1st

Source: *International Trade Statistics Yearbook*, 2002

CROPS AND INTENSIVE ANIMAL REARING

Part of the Queensland coast lies within the tropics. A wide range of crops is grown there, but the main commercial products are sugar and tropical fruits such as bananas, paw paws and pineapples. Maize and alfalfa are grown as cattle feed for ranches inland. Southwards, where the climate becomes more temperate, wheat, barley, apples, pears, and grass for hay and silage are increasingly important.

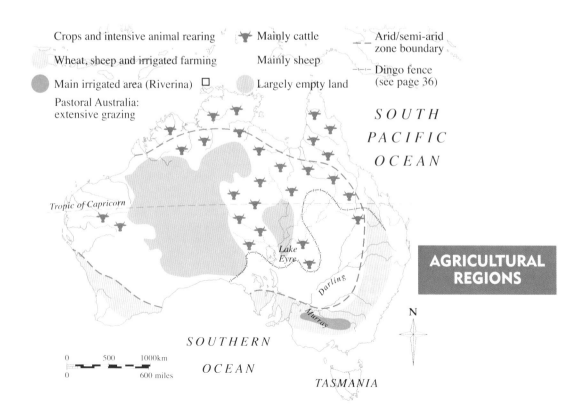

AGRICULTURAL REGIONS

Around major cities there is a zone of market gardening and dairy farms that supply the urban markets. But 60 per cent of Australia's dairy industry is concentrated in the moist, temperate districts of Victoria. Since 1970, production has doubled while the number of dairy farmers has fallen from 26,000 to fewer than 8,000.

Tasmania's climate is well suited to crops such as potatoes, apples, wheat and hay, as well as dairy and beef cattle. There are 2,700 hectares of apple orchards, producing over 50,000 tonnes of fruit per year. Most are exported, the main markets being South-east Asia and Scandinavia.

CASE STUDY
FARMING CHANGE IN NORTH QUEENSLAND

Mechanised harvesting of sugar cane near Innisfail in the far north of Queensland.

The Mareeba-Dimbula Irrigation Area (MDIA) comprises some 15,000 hectares of land in north-east Queensland, irrigated by a reservoir called Lake Tinaroo. In 1985 there were 400 farm holdings in the MDIA, and most gave tobacco as their main product. Government quota and marketing policies limited the tobacco area to 4,000 hectares, in an effort to protect local producers and maintain tobacco prices. So farmers diversified, switching to cereals such as rice and maize, vegetables including peanuts and soya beans, various fruits, and intensive beef cattle rearing.

By 2000, the farming system had changed. The irrigated area had grown by 50 per cent but tobacco had collapsed. Farmers now grew sugar cane, orchard fruits such as avocados and mangoes, and vegetables. Sugar cane covered 4,800 hectares compared with less than 300 hectares in 1985. The following three main factors explain these changes:

- **Government policy:** in 1995, after smoking-related health concerns had notably reduced demand, tobacco growing was deregulated. Quotas and price supports ended and the crop now has to compete on a global level.
- **Scale of production:** without government support, local tobacco growers are too small in scale to compete in world markets. In contrast, the Queensland sugar industry is an efficient, large-scale operation.
- **Accessibility:** improved transport and refrigeration facilities are making the MDIA less remote, so it is easier to farm perishable products. Cairns is the hub of the area.

LEADING MDIA CROPS BY VALUE, 2000 (A$ MILLION)

1. Sugar cane	33
2. Mangoes	30
3. Vegetables	21
4. Avocados	20
5. Tobacco	17

Source: *Australian Geographer*, 2001

WHEAT, SHEEP AND IRRIGATED FARMING

This area (defined on the map on page 34) supports 45 per cent of Australia's sheep and three-quarters of its cereal grains. Most farms include both wheat and sheep and some also rear cattle. The wheat belt in the south of Western Australia, with its 400–700mm of rainfall a year, makes the state Australia's leading wheat producer. More intensive cropping and animal rearing are possible along the Murray valley where irrigation systems are in operation. Except in irrigated districts, most farms are larger than 500 hectares.

RIGHT: Irrigated farmland near Cobram, on the Victoria side of the Murray valley.

PASTORAL AUSTRALIA

Extensive animal grazing dominates more than half of Australia's agricultural land. Here, stocking densities (see page 38) are very low and ranches are huge. Large sheep flocks, known as mobs, are found across the interiors of Queensland and New South Wales, where wells draw on artesian water. But in the harsher heat and aridity of Northern Territory and Western Australia, hardy cattle are more common. The approximate sheep–cattle boundary is marked by an amazing dingo fence that runs for 5,500km across South Australia and Queensland. The dingo is known to attack lambs but rarely calves, so the fence significantly reduces stock losses.

Within Australia's pastoral regions there are occasional 'islands' of irrigated land (these do not show up on the generalised map on page 34). The best example is the Ord River Irrigation Area, at the tropical northern tip of Western Australia, with its main crops of sugar and cotton.

RIGHT: The dingo, Australia's wild dog, poses a serious threat to grazing sheep.

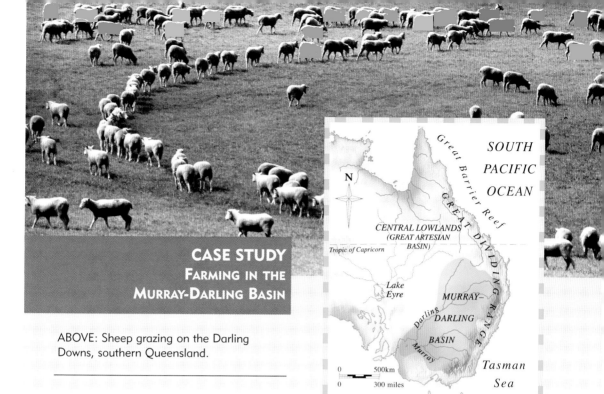

CASE STUDY
FARMING IN THE
MURRAY-DARLING BASIN

SOUTH
PACIFIC
OCEAN

N

Great Barrier Reef

GREAT DIVIDING RANGE

CENTRAL LOWLANDS
(GREAT ARTESIAN
BASIN)

Tropic of Capricorn

*Lake
Eyre*

MURRAY–
Darling DARLING
Murray BASIN

*Tasman
Sea*

0   500km
0   300 miles

ABOVE: Sheep grazing on the Darling
Downs, southern Queensland.

The Murray-Darling Basin (MDB) covers an area four times larger than the UK. It has a wide network of permanent streams, plus many seasonal tributaries. Average annual rainfall ranges from 200mm in the north-west to over 1,600mm in the Snowy Mountains.

More than 85 per cent of the MDB's river water is now used. This includes transfers outside the basin to supply the population of Adelaide. To cope with increasing demand, 25 billion cubic metres of water a year are transferred into the headwaters of the Murray and Murrumbidgee rivers via the Snowy Mountains Project (see page 32). During drought periods, the Murray is often just a trickle at its mouth east of Adelaide.

Towards the north and west of the MDB, rainfall declines and the dry season extends. Farms are large and extensive sheep grazing is common. On the hills and plains of the Wimmera in western Victoria, farms average 500–800 hectares and specialise in wheat and sheep or cattle and sheep. To the north, over the Darling Downs of southern Queensland, holdings are at least 5,000 hectares and extensive sheep grazing dominates.

This trend is interrupted in two ways – firstly where rivers supply water for irrigation, and secondly where groundwater can be drawn from wells. In the MDB approximately

14,000km² are irrigated. The largest area is the flat Riverina region of southern New South Wales. Here, agriculture is intensive – fruit farms, vineyards and animal fattening units may be less than 200 hectares but highly productive. The upper Darling Basin, in southern Queensland, overlaps the Great Artesian Basin. Here, groundwater is pumped from wells to improve pastures for sheep.

WATER ISSUES

Concern is rising about water quantities in the MDB, because groundwater stores refill very slowly. During the twentieth century, levels in parts of the Great Artesian Basin fell by up to 120m, showing that more water was being taken out than was coming in.

Along the River Murray, water quality is a problem, too. Removal of eucalyptus woodland and scrub has caused serious salination (build-up of salts) in the soils. Pastures and crop yields are being affected and some of the salts run off into rivers. In addition, farmers have been increasing their use of chemical sprays and fertilisers. Some of these run into the rivers. The combination of natural salts and introduced chemicals is causing serious water pollution along the middle and lower Murray.

GRAZING THE OUTBACK

Across the vast, dry expanses of much of Western Australia and Northern Territory, farming means cattle ranching. Cattle stations, as the ranches are known, are huge. They average at least 50,000 hectares, with the largest over 1 million hectares. They need to be huge because the cattle have to move great distances to find grazing and water. Thus, stocking densities (the number of animals per unit area) are very low. One station in Northern Territory runs 50,000 cattle and perhaps 20,000 calves on a massive 1.25 million hectares. This is a stocking density of approximately one animal per 18 hectares.

Human population densities in the Outback, as this area is known, are very low, too. For example, in more than 1.5 million km^2 of northern and central Western Australia there are only 90,000 people, including 16,000 Aborigines. Settlements may be 200km apart, and the homesteads are very isolated. Many children and students learn via television, radio and computer-based programmes, or go away to boarding schools and colleges. Families rely on Flying Doctor services for medical treatment. Most homesteads house the rancher's family, with accommodation for the stockmen and their families. Many Aborigines are valuable stockmen because they understand and can tolerate the harsh environment. A single homestead may be home for up to 30 people.

The majority of the land in the Outback is still owned by the government or is under aboriginal title rights. As a result, cattle stations lease most of their land, although the long lets make it almost like ownership. An increasing amount of land is leased by large US and Asian companies.

RIGHT: Many Outback areas are so remote that light aircraft are the only practical means of transport in an emergency.
BELOW: Wooleen sheep station, Western Australia, covers more than 200,000 hectares.

CASE STUDY
THE DRYSDALE RIVER STATION
(WESTERN AUSTRALIA)

Ranchers use horses, backed up by trucks and often helicopters, to round up cattle roaming widely across the dusty red Outback terrain.

The Drysdale River cattle station covers 260,000 hectares of the rugged Kimberley Plateau in north-west Western Australia. The ranchers own the animals and machinery, but they lease the buildings and land from the government. The cattle wander across wide areas to find enough food from the sparse vegetation. During the 'Wet' – the regional name for the summer monsoon – the Drysdale River becomes a broad, shallow flood for several weeks. The water submerges all surfaced roads and the station is cut off, except by air. Cattle have to survive on pieces of higher ground. But vegetation sprouts quickly when the floods recede, providing valuable fodder for the hungry animals.

Once a year the cattle are mustered (rounded up). Helicopters are hired to help the four-wheel-drive trucks and the stockmen riding on horses. In the vast, rugged terrain, some animals may not be found – the rancher is not even sure how many cattle he has, but he estimates a total of around 7,000. Each year about 600–700 cows and bulls are sold, mostly for export as hamburger beef.

Wyndham is the nearest town, nearly 200km away, with a hospital, school and other services. Trips for supplies are made every few weeks. Homestead families are very self-reliant and may not see other people for weeks. Younger children learn at home through the School of the Air, and then go away to boarding school. The Flying Doctor comes for medical checks, but serious illness or injury means a stay in Wyndham and, for major surgery, patients need to go to Perth.

RURAL CHANGE

Since 1970, Australian agriculture has changed. The restructuring is having serious effects on rural communities. For example, numbers of farmers and farm workers fell by 16 per cent in Western Australia between 1990 and 2000. In 2001 alone, 2,000 farms closed down. By 2020, full-time farm work will probably make up less than one in four jobs in many rural districts. Farms are becoming larger but fewer, and employing fewer people. Between 1981 and 2001, 40 per cent of rural districts lost population. It is younger people who tend to move away.

CAUSES OF FARMING CHANGE

- Less protection and funding from the government.
- Increased competition in global markets.
- Changes in demand and fluctuating prices.
- Improved transport and marketing organisation.

TOWNS IN DECLINE

Agricultural and social changes affect the network of towns that grew up as service centres for rural communities. Many are losing their traditional functions and they need to adapt to survive. The combination of big-city growth, changing agriculture and rising expectations is creating major problems throughout the more remote parts of Australia. Population densities are too low to sustain services or to provide a range of career opportunities.

An increasing number of Australia's remote rural towns are in danger of decline as they lose population to the main cities.

CASE STUDY
CHANGES IN THE RURAL TOWN OF LEETON (NEW SOUTH WALES)

In the remote rural towns of Australia, most industries are closely tied to local agriculture. As agriculture changes, so must the industries, if the towns are to survive.

Leeton is a town of 6,500 people, with a surrounding rural population of 5,500. The district lies in the Murrumbidgee Irrigation Area of southern New South Wales. The main crops grown are fruits, wheat, rice and animal fodder. Leeton's industries are based on supplying the farmers and processing and distributing their products.

In 1994 the Letona Co-operative Cannery closed. This was one of the town's oldest and largest businesses, set up in 1921 and run by a co-operative of 240 local fruit growers. The main fruits canned were peaches, apricots and pears. The cannery employed up to 700 people, many seasonal. Wages to workers and payments to growers and haulage companies put more than A$20 million into the local economy each year. So the effect of the cannery's closure was, at first, serious. In 1995, 25 per cent of the shops and business premises in the main street were empty.

The chief causes of the closure were increased competition, changing tastes by consumers, insufficient funds to modernise the plant, and a reduction in government financial support.

Agriculture in the district has now adapted to changing markets – tomatoes, citrus fruits, rice and grapes are replacing the peaches and apricots. Animal feed crops are increasing to support the growing number of animal fattening enterprises. Leeton lies close to one of Australia's main wine-producing regions, so vineyards are also expanding.

Leeton is trying hard to further diversify its economy. The arrival of a company making air conditioning and hospital equipment is one example of this. Leeton lies close to the main Sydney–Melbourne road corridor, so it is well placed for transporting components and finished products. One problem Leeton faces is competition from the larger town of Griffith, located only 25km to the west, which offers a wider range of services.

LEETON'S MAIN EMPLOYERS, 1999

	EMPLOYEES	DATE ESTABLISHED
Local and state government	500	Before 1970
Cattle feedlots and abattoirs	500	Since 1990
Rice Growers Co-operative	400	Before 1970
Air conditioning & hospital equipment	120	Since 1990
Cereal and breakfast food processors	100	Since 1990
Citrus fruit processors	60	Since 1990
Engineering	50	1980s
Hay & animal feed merchants	25	1980s
Steel fabricators (farm & industrial buildings)	25	1970s

Source: *Australian Geographer*, 2000

Wool is still one of Australia's major exports, but its economic value is declining.

There was a popular saying that the Australian economy was 'carried on the back of a sheep and in a miner's barrow'. This referred to the time when the country's business was mainly in primary products – wool, meat, sugar, timber, coal and other minerals. Today, Australia's economy is much broader.

Australia is still one of the world's major sources of primary products (raw materials). But in recent years, the export of secondary (manufactured) goods has brought in more money. At the same time, the leading imports are manufactured products such as machinery, vehicles and telecommunications equipment.

ECONOMIC STRUCTURE, 2004 (% GDP CONTRIBUTIONS)

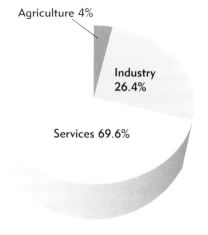

Agriculture 4%

Industry 26.4%

Services 69.6%

Source: CIA World Factbook, 2006

AUSTRALIA'S EXPORTS, 2001 (% OF TOTAL)

Manufacturing	45
Services	23
Mining	20
Agriculture, forestry, fishing	8
Other products	4

Source: International Trade Statistics Yearbook, 2002

THE JOB MARKET

The global economy prospered during much of the 1990s and this benefited Australia's industries. In 2006, there were 10.1 million jobs and unemployment fell to 5 per cent (from almost 11 per cent in 1993). Figures vary from region to region. For example, in 2006 Victoria had the country's lowest unemployment level – 5.1 per cent – while in Tasmania about 6.6 per cent were without a job. More than one in five of Australia's workers are immigrants.

CHANGING TRADE

Because modern Australia developed as part of the British Empire, the UK was for a long time Australia's main trading partner. Britain's Commonwealth Preference policy meant that Australia's wool, meat and minerals had low import tariffs. However, from the 1950s, other countries became increasingly competitive. The most important change occurred when Britain joined the European Community (EC) – now the European Union (EU) – in 1973.

The Commonwealth Preference advantages were phased out during the 1960s. In response, Australia sought other markets, and looked increasingly to the USA for exports and imports. More investment came too, from US businesses such as multinational oil and mining companies. This coincided with the Australian government's move to privatise industries and reduce government subsidies.

The Sydney skyline exhibits the importance of international businesses to Australia's economy.

Since 1980, a third wave of change has seen the Australian economy forge more links with industrial east and South-east Asia. Japan is now the main trading partner and provides the leading market for Australia's coal, iron ore and pulpwood. Australia is today firmly tied to the Asian–Pacific market.

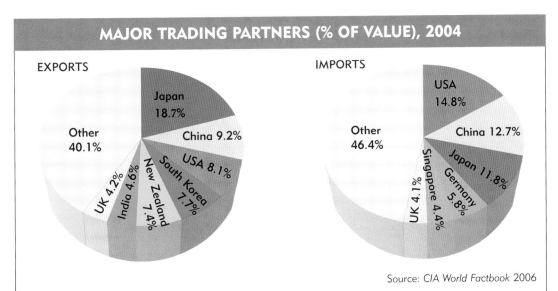

MAJOR TRADING PARTNERS (% OF VALUE), 2004

EXPORTS

- Japan 18.7%
- Other 40.1%
- China 9.2%
- USA 8.1%
- UK 4.2%
- India 4.6%
- New Zealand 7.4%
- South Korea 7.7%

IMPORTS

- USA 14.8%
- Other 46.4%
- China 12.7%
- Japan 11.8%
- Germany 5.8%
- Singapore 4.4%
- UK 4.1%

Source: *CIA World Factbook* 2006

Visitors to the Sovereign Hill Outdoor Museum in Ballarat, Victoria, can pan for gold in the reconstruction of an 1850s mining township.

MINERALS AND MINING

Australia's mineral resources have been vital to the economy for more than 150 years. Gold was discovered at Ballarat (Victoria) in 1851 and the following gold rush helped to treble Australia's population. During the twentieth century, global industrialisation boosted markets for iron ore, non-ferrous metals, fossil fuels and uranium. Growing wealth heightened demand for precious metals such as gold, and stones such as diamonds. Improved technology helped mining to grow in scale and in remoteness of location. Today Australia supplies 95 per cent of the world's opals, has the largest diamond mine and boasts the largest lead-zinc deposit.

PEAKS AND PITFALLS

Like all industries, mining is affected by world economic changes. For example, prices fell during the 1960–1990 period and Australia suffered financially. In contrast, the boom years of the 1990s saw mining grow rapidly, benefiting mineral-rich states such as Queensland and Western Australia.

One constant issue is that modern mining in remote locations is expensive and has a limited lifespan. It is also a capital-intensive industry, creating relatively few jobs compared with the amount of investment put in – fewer than 50,000 people are employed in the country's mining industry as a whole.

Mount Isa in north-west Queensland is Australia's largest underground mine and the leading world producer of silver, lead, copper and zinc.

Mining is the most important industry in Western Australia. In 2004, minerals and oil made up 80 per cent of the state's exports and 51,958 people were employed in the minerals and petroleum industries. Much of the growth has been recent – in 1980 the state gold output was only 11 tonnes but by 2004 it was 164 tonnes. Mining has made Perth, the state capital, a boom city with more than 1 million inhabitants.

A specially-constructed village 8km from the Argyle diamond mine houses all workers.

Western Australia's mines are widely scattered, often in remote places. The Pilbara district, 1,000km north of Perth, has the richest collection of minerals including iron ore, gold, diamonds, zinc and bauxite. They are shipped through the specialised ports of Dampier and Port Hedland. During the 1990s, a large offshore oil and gas field was developed with onshore facilities at Karratha.

GHOST TOWNS

Minerals are finite, non-renewable resources, so any individual mine has a limited lifespan despite the expense of its development. The Anaconda Nickel Corporation has recently spent A$1 billion at their new Murrin Murrin operation in the south. It will produce 45,000 tonnes of nickel and 3,000 tonnes of cobalt a year with a workforce of 600 people. But it will last only 25–30 years. Mining creates towns, such as Kalgoorlie with a population of 28,000, but they may become 'ghost towns' when mining finishes.

FIFO

One answer to this problem in remote locations is the 'Fly-in/Fly-out' (FiFo) system. Accommodation and facilities are provided for mine workers, but not for their families. Workers 'commute' by air, usually for two-week spells at the mine. This reduces the cost of building towns that are only likely to last short-term. The remote Argyle mine in the Kimberley region is a good example. It is the world's largest diamond mine, opened in 1985, but it is expected to close in 2008. Most of the workers are flown the 1,400km from Perth, while their families remain in the city. By 2001 there were at least 50 mines operating this system, involving one-fifth of all mine workers.

WEALTH FROM MINERALS IN WESTERN AUSTRALIA, 2004

	A$ BILLION
1. Iron ore	6.2
2. Nickel	3.2
3. Alumina*	3.2
4. Gold	2.9

*Alumina is the main component of bauxite, the ore from which aluminium is processed

Source: *Western Australia Mineral & Petroleum Digest*, 2004

EXAMPLES OF MINES IN WESTERN AUSTRALIA

(Au) Gold
(Fe) Iron ore
(Ni) Nickel
(Al) Bauxite
(D) Diamonds
Natural gas

MANUFACTURING AND SERVICES

In 1970, one in four Australian workers were in the manufacturing industries. Now there are only one in eight. Because factories have become more efficient and productive, output has grown despite the decreasing workforce.

Holden cars being assembled at the Melbourne plant. The Australian Holden Company is now part of the massive US firm, General Motors.

Manufacturing industries today produce 11 per cent of the country's GDP and a substantial 43 per cent of its exports.

THRIVING OR FALLING

From the 1970s, globalisation and competition from other countries hit some of Australia's industries hard. For example, by 2001 employment in the textiles and clothing industry had dropped to less than 60,000, from almost three times that in 1971. In vehicle manufacture, the Australian Holden corporation was swallowed up by US General Motors and Japan's Mitsubishi.

CASE STUDY
MAKING KITCHEN EQUIPMENT

In 1975 there were 27 companies in Australia making refrigerators, cookers and washing machines. All were in the state capitals, except for one – the Email company – which was based in Orange, a town of 20,000 people inland from Sydney. By 1999, there were only four such companies. Email bought up businesses in Sydney, Melbourne and Adelaide and now has 60 per cent of the domestic market. It has survived competition from foreign imports by reorganising its production – a specialised factory in Orange makes refrigerators, while other products are made in Sydney and Melbourne. Email is now the largest employer in Orange, with 2,000 workers, and is the main reason why the town's population has grown to over 30,000.

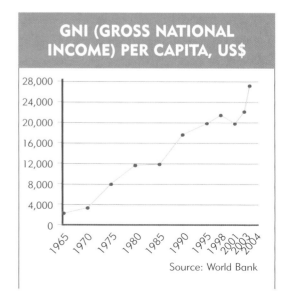

GNI (GROSS NATIONAL INCOME) PER CAPITA, US$

Source: World Bank

Harvesting grapes for wine production, one of Australia's rapidly growing industries.

In contrast, the food and drink industries are expanding. Castlemaine and Foster's beers are sold worldwide. Since 1990, Australia's production and export of wines has doubled. The manufacture of mechanical and electronic parts is also growing, as are heavy industries such as steel works.

During the past 25 years, the following changes have occurred:

- More companies have become part of multinational corporations.
- Production has concentrated in fewer, larger, more specialised factories.
- Many companies have left core cities for the suburbs and regional towns and cities.

Between 1990 and 2000, manufacturing jobs in Sydney and Melbourne declined by 10 per cent. But in the outer suburbs and regional towns, they grew by more than 15 per cent. Newcastle and Wollongong, to either side of Sydney, are important centres for metals and machinery. Vehicle assembly plants and component suppliers cluster outside Melbourne. Around 70 per cent of all Australia's manufacturing jobs are in the Sydney–Melbourne region.

THE SERVICES REVOLUTION

Over the past 30 years, the rapid growth of service industries has changed the structure of Australia's economy. These industries now provide 69.6 per cent of the country's GDP, up from 52 per cent in 1980. Three in every four jobs fall within the services category.

- 37 per cent of service sector employees have professional, administrative, managerial and technical jobs.
- Between 1985 and 2002, jobs in financial, property and business services doubled to almost 1.4 million.
- During the 1990s, jobs in service industries grew by an average of 19 per cent a year, compared with 4 per cent in other industries.
- 'Knowledge-based' industries, such as financial services, computer programming and legal services, have provided half of all jobs created since 1970, and they now generate 50 per cent of GDP.
- The Australian film and television industry is now a major global competitor.
- Service industries provide increasing job opportunities for women.

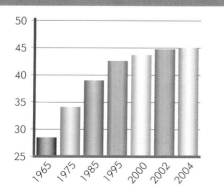

FEMALE LABOUR FORCE (% OF TOTAL)

Source: World Bank

ENERGY AND FUEL PRODUCTION

Australia used twice as much energy in 2001 as it did in 1971. This was due to a combination of population growth, economic expansion and rising standards of living – electricity demand rose by 65 per cent between 1981 and 2001. New South Wales and Victoria are responsible for almost 60 per cent of the country's energy consumption.

More than 90 per cent of Australia's energy comes from fossil fuels. This is not surprising considering the country's rich mineral fuel resources – only oil needs to be imported. Almost two-thirds of all electricity is generated by coal-fired power stations. Yet, over half of the coal mined is exported. The recent exploitation of large natural gas fields off the coast of Western Australia explains why production of this fuel has rocketed.

COAL

Australia is a major producer and the world's leading exporter of coal. In 2004, out of an output of 378 million tonnes, 219 million tonnes were exported. The main coalfields are close to the coast, so they are convenient for shipping to international markets.

An aerial view of the coal terminal at Newcastle, just north of Sydney on the coast of New South Wales. Coal is delivered here from inland mines and loaded onto ships for export.

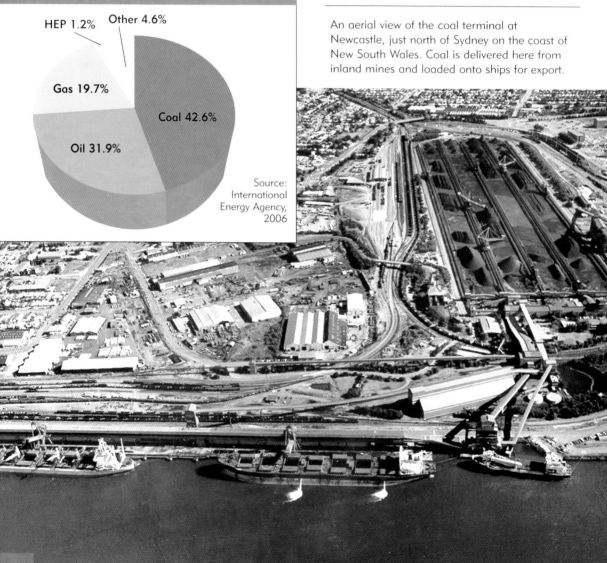

ENERGY SUPPLY, 2003

HEP 1.2% Other 4.6% Gas 19.7% Coal 42.6% Oil 31.9%

Source: International Energy Agency, 2006

48

FOSSIL FUELS OUTPUT, 1994 AND 2004

	1994	2004
Coal (Mtoe*)	123.3	199.4
Oil (million tonnes)	30.6	26.9
Gas (Mtoe*)	25.3	31.7

* = million tonnes of oil equivalent
Source: *BP Statistical Review of World Energy 2005*

Because Australia relies on fossil fuels for energy and export, the Australian government was reluctant to sign the 1991 Kyoto Treaty on reducing atmospheric pollution. Australia has one of the world's highest emission rates per head of population. The target of the 1991 Treaty was to reduce emissions by at least 8 per cent by 2010. Between 1991 and 2002, CO_2 emissions in Australia *increased* by 35.5 per cent.

TRAFFIC AND TRANSPORT

Australian transport is dominated by two factors – the huge size of the country and the clustered population. In the cities, there are more than 12 million motor vehicles for fewer than 20 million people. Traffic densities and commuter surges are similar to those in the UK and there are enough people to support public transport systems. However, when you

A 'road train' rolls along the lonely Victoria Highway in a remote part of Western Australia.

drive beyond the cities, the lack of traffic is striking. Much of Australia is very empty and has few surfaced roads. There may be 400km between petrol stations or settlements. You will cover 14,900km if you drive around Australia on the main highway – without even going to Tasmania! It is very expensive to maintain the 330,000km of surfaced road.

A rail network along the east coast and west–east links Melbourne, Adelaide and Perth. In 2002, a south–north line between Adelaide and Darwin was completed. Railways are efficient for freight but too slow for most people – it takes a train two days to get from Perth to Adelaide, for example. Air travel is the obvious way to overcome distances – you can fly from Perth to Sydney in five hours – but there are too few passengers to keep fares low. The government has reduced its funding and internal airlines find it difficult to survive. The hope is that as international tourism and Australia's population continue to grow, passenger volumes will increase. Meanwhile, telecommunications remains a vital industry.

TELECOMMUNICATIONS DATA PER 1,000 PEOPLE, 2004

Mainline phones	541
Mobile phones	818
Internet users	646

Source: World Bank

CONSERVATION, LEISURE AND TOURISM

Salt-ravaged agricultural land in the Wimmera District, north-west Victoria.

Australians are very proud of their country. They love their unique environment but are increasingly aware of how they are affecting it. Conservation has become an important issue, with the aim of reducing the damage caused by industry, agriculture and, increasingly, leisure and tourism.

IMPACTS OF AGRICULTURE

A recent survey estimated that 50 per cent of pasture and 30 per cent of arable land showed noticeable signs of degradation – in other words, it was becoming less productive. Sheep and cattle grazing, even in low numbers, can quickly reduce the sparse vegetation of arid areas. This leads to erosion of the soil and further loss of vegetation.

SOME ENVIRONMENTAL THREATS

- Urban sprawl
- Intensification of agriculture
- Deforestation
- Increasing demands for minerals and water
- Introduced species
- Growth of leisure and tourism

In more intensely farmed, moister regions, soil salination has become a major problem. The main cause is the clearance of woodland, whose vegetation would normally maintain the balance of salts in the soils. Without the trees, natural salts build up to unusually high levels. This leads to poor plant growth and crop failure. Some of the salts are also flushed into streams, which then contaminate urban water supplies and irrigation systems. State governments are encouraging reforestation projects to reduce the threat of salination.

IMPACTS OF FORESTRY

Dense forests in Australia are limited to the upland fringes and Tasmania. For many years, logging companies have exploited these valuable resources – one-third of the old-growth forests have been cleared or disturbed. Over the past 30 years, environmental groups and government agencies have campaigned against this. In Queensland, logging of the tropical rainforests is now severely controlled, but this has meant loss of jobs and income.

ABOVE: Logs from a regrowth forest in the Styx Valley, southern Tasmania, are tied down for transport to a pulp and paper mill.
LEFT: The destruction of eucalyptus forests poses a serious threat to the koala which depends on eucalyptus leaves for food and moisture.

Western Tasmania is a magnificent landscape of forested mountains and deep river valleys. For several decades, environmental groups have fought to conserve this natural beauty. In the 1980s they prevented the building of a large dam and reservoir for HEP in the spectacular gorge of the Franklin River. Several national parks have been combined into the high-conservation Tasmania Wilderness World Heritage Area (TWWHA). But despite this, large-scale logging continues.

CONSERVATION OR ECONOMY?

Tasmania is the world's second-largest exporter of woodchips, after the USA. At present almost all of the output comes from old-growth forests. These precious temperate rainforests have more plant and animal species than any other ecosystem in Australia. Yet in 2003, despite some protection within the TWWHA, an area the size of 15 football pitches was being cleared each day. The logging and woodchip industry is important to the state economy. It employs over 5,000 people and demand is growing. In 2006, Tasmania's unemployment rate was 6.6 per cent (down from 12 per cent in recent years) and young people have left for Melbourne and Sydney. If logging declines, unemployment will rise. There is debate over which is more important – conservation of the island, or its economy.

THREATS TO NATIVE SPECIES

The spread of farming and forestry has ruined habitats for many native creatures – the koala, for example, eats only eucalyptus foliage, so woodland clearance is fatal. The introduction of new species, intentionally and by accident, is another serious problem. All major farm animals and crops have been brought from other continents. There are also domestic and wild creatures – horses, cats, dogs, foxes and rabbits – all from Europe. Because many of Australia's species – such as koalas, wombats and echidnas (spiny anteaters) – have not developed ways of defending themselves from introduced species, they are easy targets for foxes and wild (feral) cats. In turn, because of the good food supply, the intruder species have thrived and multiplied. Today, one of the main aims in national parks and other protected reserves is to remove all introduced species and provide safe habitats for native species.

ANIMAL PLAGUES

Rabbits are hardy animals that breed rapidly and destroy grazing pastures. Since arriving in Australia, their population has exploded to hundreds of millions and the government has declared them a national plague. Attempts to control numbers include shooting, poisoning and rabbit-proof fencing such as the 2,000km fence across Western Australia.

The impacts of introduced species continue. In the 1930s, cane toads were introduced to control an insect that was attacking Queensland's sugar cane plants. Unfortunately, the project failed. The toads have since multiplied dramatically and become a widespread pest, harming native ecosystems and even injuring humans with their poisonous bite.

BELOW: Rabbit 'plagues' devastate grazing land.
MAIN PICTURE: Victoria's Grampians National Park is a protected area of great natural beauty.

AUSTRALIANS AT PLAY

Outdoor recreation on land and in water plays an important part in Australian culture. For a country with fewer than 20 million people, Australia has impressive large-scale sporting achievements. It is a world leader in cricket, rugby, tennis, sailing, surfing and swimming and has many top quality facilities, including the National Sports Academy. The success of the 2000 Olympic Games in Sydney illustrates the country's sporting pride and enthusiasm.

A favourable climate and spacious suburban homes encourage outdoor 'barbie and beer' lifestyles. Most of Australia's population live within 20km of the coast, so beaches and water sports – such as surfing, windsurfing and sailing – are very popular. The annual Sydney–Hobart yacht race is a leading world event. More than 30 per cent of people take part in some form of water-based activity.

On land, hiking or 'bush-bashing' is popular. All states have national parks – with camping facilities, trails and wilderness areas – and these attract more than 5 million people a year. Some, such as the Royal Sydney National Park,

Queensland's Fraser Island can be explored by off-road vehicle, but access areas are restricted to protect threatened habitats and species.

are close to cities. Others can be reached for weekend breaks, for example Wilson's Promontory National Park – a three hour drive from Melbourne. Some, such as the Kakadu National Park in Northern Territory, are far more remote and require long-distance travel.

Recently, the development of four-wheel-drive vehicles and high-tech camping equipment has encouraged more Australians to explore remote parts of their country. For example, in 1980 there were fewer than 20,000 visitors to Queensland's Fraser Island. Today, more than 250,000 people flock there per year, since the upgrading of ferry facilities and the introduction of off-road vehicles.

People are becoming more concerned about the impact that this growth in outdoor recreation will have on the environment.

Along the coasts, there are strong planning controls because of pressures to build more marinas and develop more beaches. To help protect the fragile Fraser Island environment, a zoning plan has been introduced, restricting the use of off-road vehicles to certain areas. Many other national parks have similar zoning policies. In Wilson's Promontory National Park, all major camping facilities are concentrated in one location. Elsewhere in the park there are no surfaced roads and only 'primitive' small-scale campsites. The aim is to protect the delicate habitats and endangered species such as koalas and wombats.

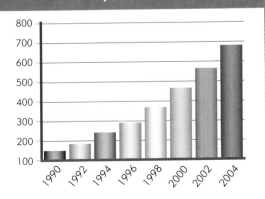

PERSONAL COMPUTERS PER 1,000 PEOPLE

Source: World Bank

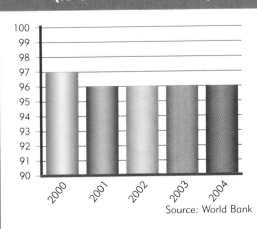

TELEVISION SET OWNERSHIP (% OF HOUSEHOLDS)

Source: World Bank

Adventurous tourists are increasingly attracted by exploration into remote Outback areas such as this bush camp in South Australia.

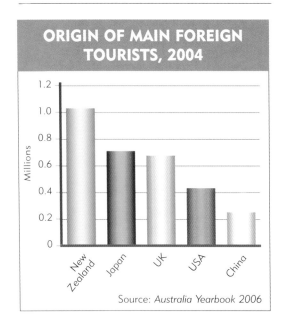

ORIGIN OF MAIN FOREIGN TOURISTS, 2004

Source: *Australia Yearbook 2006*

TOURISM: A BOOM INDUSTRY

Australia is becoming increasingly popular as a tourist destination. In 2004 there were approximately 5.2 million visitors to Australia, bringing in A\$26.15 billion – 2.8 per cent of GDP. More than a third of Australia's tourists come from Asia, especially Japan. The large numbers from New Zealand show the close connections between the two countries.

REASONS FOR TOURISM
The majority of Australia's visitors are holidaymakers, and a further fifth are visiting friends and relatives. This is not surprising when you think how many immigrants live in Australia (see page 22). New South Wales attracts 40 per cent of all foreign visitors, with Sydney the main centre. Queensland, with its alluring environment, glorious coastline and

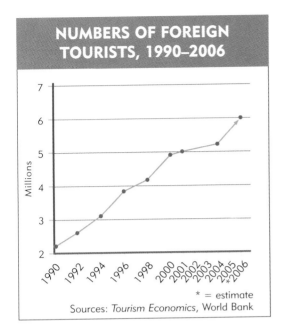

NUMBERS OF FOREIGN TOURISTS, 1990–2006

* = estimate
Sources: *Tourism Economics*, World Bank

in luxury beach resorts; there are specialist wildlife trips and large-scale package tours. Australia is popular with gap year students, who often go backpacking for several months, staying in hostels and finding temporary jobs. At the other extreme, most Japanese tourists travel on mass package tours, making brief visits to a small number of famous places.

DOMESTIC TOURISM
Australians take at least 70 million business and pleasure trips a year within their own country. Most business travellers fly between the big cities. Seaside areas, especially Queensland's Gold Coast and the Great Barrier Reef, are the most popular holiday destinations. Coastal and mountain districts within weekend reach of the big cities are also growing rapidly. South of Perth in Western Australia, the population of the Cape Naturaliste to Cape Leeuwin area has recently increased by 50 per cent. In 2000, tourism projects worth A$80 million were under construction there, including holiday homes for Perth families.

the Great Barrier Reef, gets 25 per cent of all 'visitor nights' (one visitor night = one person staying for one night).

Tourists are drawn by Australia's superb variety, both in nature and in culture. There are adventure treks to the Outback and stays

CASE STUDY
TOURISM COMES TO CAIRNS

In 1976, Cairns, on the coast of northern Queensland, had a population of 57,000 and its economy was based on agriculture. A small number of tourists travelled there, mainly by boat. In 2006, the population had more than doubled – largely due to a tourism boom. Today, a third of all foreign visitors to Australia include Cairns on their itinerary. The prime attractions are the Great Barrier Reef (see pages 56–57) and the wildlife-rich tropical rainforests.

Cairns and its neighbouring coastline have 10,000 hotel rooms, 3,000 holiday

rental flats, 3,000 beds in hostels and sites for 7,500 caravans. Yearly, around 500,000 international visitors and 400,000 Australians stay an average of six nights in the region. Vital elements in this expansion have been:
• The opening of Cairns International Airport to take wide-bodied jets (1983).
• The introduction of high-speed catamarans, allowing day-trips to the Great Barrier Reef (early 1980s).
• The use of four-wheel-drive vehicles to make tracks into the rainforests (1990s).
• The encouragement of foreign investment (for example, 40 per cent of investment since 1980 has been from Japan and South-east Asia).

TOURISM AND THE GREAT BARRIER REEF

The Great Barrier Reef is the world's largest coral reef system and perhaps Australia's most famous natural attraction. It runs for 2,000km off the east coast of Queensland and has 3,000 separate reefs, islands and cays. In total, it covers an area greater than the states of Tasmania and Victoria combined.

THE RICHNESS OF THE REEF

A coral is a plant-like animal that lives in close combination with certain types of algae. As the corals die, their skeletons gradually make up a limestone platform on which the colourful living coral sits. The Great Barrier Reef has built up slowly over 10,000 years. It is the most diverse and productive ecosystem in the world. There are 400 types of coral, 1,500 species of fish, 4,000 types of mollusc and six of the seven known species of turtle. In every hectare of water there may be 100,000 fish.

THE SENSITIVE REEF

Corals need the sea water to be at least 18°C, and clear so that sunlight can penetrate. The algae on which the corals depend need sunlight to photosynthesise food. So living coral is generally found in shallow water, less than 20m deep. Like the corals themselves, many species that live on the reef are highly specialised. They need constant conditions in order to survive and are very sensitive to changes in the reef environment.

THREATS TO THE REEF

The reef is very attractive, especially for commercial fishing and tourism. In 2002, tourism brought some A$4 billion to Queensland's economy. In 1990 the reef received 2.5 million tourists and by 2000 this had grown to 4 million, 60 per cent of whom were foreign visitors. Most visitors are on day-trips from harbours such as Cairns and Port Douglas. They fish, snorkel, scuba-dive or observe from glass-bottomed boats. Increasing numbers of islands have luxury resorts, marinas and even airstrips. The continuing pressure to bring in more tourists is just one of the serious threats to the fragile reef.

MAIN THREATS TO THE REEF

- Pollution from boats, growing coastal towns and agricultural chemicals.
- Silt from local deforestation and mangrove clearance, making the water cloudy.
- Direct impacts by increasing numbers of tourists and boats.
- Growing pressures from commercial and recreational fishing.
- Intrusive species such as the 'crown of thorns' starfish which eat the live coral, preventing regrowth (during the 1980s a population explosion of this species caused extensive coral damage).
- Global warming (and hence rising water temperatures) which causes coral bleaching as individual corals die away (in 2002, 60 per cent of the reef area showed some bleaching damage).

The colourful reef, teeming with marine life, is a great attraction for divers. It is a rich but fragile ecosystem.

MANAGING THE REEF

The reef now lies within the Great Barrier Reef Marine Park (GBRMP). The park's aim is *'to provide for the protection, wise use, understanding and enjoyment of the Great Barrier Reef in perpetuity'*. This gives managers the difficult task of balancing vital conservation measures with optimum use of the park.

The park plan is based on a zoning system that controls the way each area is used. For example, all commercial businesses must have a licence, which is hard to get. This allows them to operate in certain zones, but limits what they can do and when and where they can go. To protect the most precious and fragile areas, a series of 'green zones' excludes tourists and fishing boats from

Heron Island is one of three coral cays on the Great Barrier Reef that have tourist facilities. It is world famous for turtle breeding.

almost 5 per cent of the park. In 2003 the managers introduced a plan to extend these conservation zones to 30 per cent of the park.

AUSTRALIA'S FUTURE

The Great Barrier Reef sums up some key questions facing Australians about their future: how to use their resources and how to conserve them. They are proud of their young country and its wonderful environment. At the same time they are increasingly aware of both the benefits and the threats of increasing populations and continued economic expansion. They want their population and economy to grow, but they are concerned about losing control of this growth. For example, how can they reap the benefits of the developing markets of eastern Asia without being swamped by them? The government faces challenging times, but the potential rewards for Australia are great.

Aquifer A layer of underground rock that soaks up and stores water.

Arid A term used to describe an environment that generally receives less than 250mm annual rainfall.

Birth rate The number of children born in a year per 1,000 population.

Boom city A city that experiences rapid economic growth.

Cay A small, flat sand island overlying a coral reef.

Colony (political) A territory that is taken over and ruled by another country.

Counterurbanisation The movement of people from cities to live in smaller towns and rural settlements.

Depression A low-pressure atmospheric system.

Dingo The wild dog of Australia.

Diversification Broadening an economy or business by adding new activities.

Drainage basin The total area that contributes water to a river.

Ecosystem A system that represents the relationships within a community of living things (plants and animals) and between this community and their non-living environment. An ecosystem can be as small as a pond or as large as the Earth.

Emigration The movement of people away from a country, city, or other place, to live elsewhere.

Erosion The wearing away of soil or rock by the forces of nature (such as wind and rain) or the actions of people (such as deforestation).

Estuary The mouth of a river where it broadens into the sea.

Federation A country that is divided into regions (states) whose individual governments take greater control of their own affairs with a lesser role for the central government.

Fertility rate The average number of children a woman gives birth to during her lifetime.

Flash flood A sudden flood in a dry stream bed, caused by a heavy rainstorm.

Fodder crop A crop grown to be fed to animals.

GDP (Gross Domestic Product) The monetary value of goods and services produced by a country in a single year.

Gentrification The process by which older, run-down urban neighbourhoods are improved by relatively affluent people moving in.

Glacial trough A deep valley, often U-shaped, carved by a glacier.

Globalisation When large corporations base themselves in a number of different countries.

GNI (Gross National Income) Sometimes called Gross National Product or GNP, this is the monetary value of goods and services produced by a country, plus any earnings from overseas, in a single year.

Homeland The traditional territory of an indigenous group of people.

HEP (Hydroelectric power) Electricity generated by water as it passes through turbines.

Immigration The movement of people into a country, city, or other place, to live.

Intensification Farming more intensively to increase productivity per unit area of land.

Irrigation The controlled addition of water to agricultural land to improve plant growth.

Marsupial A type of mammal whose females use a pouch to carry their immature young.

Monsoon The seasonal period of heavy rains, or the heavy rains themselves, experienced in a tropical climate.

Mortality rate The number of people who die in a year per 1,000 population.

Mulla mulla A wild, flowering shrub native to parts of Australia.

Multinational corporation A large business that has operations in a number of countries.

Natural increase The excess of births over deaths.

Old-growth forest An original forest, before any logging or replanting has taken place.

Outback A general term for the remote, sparsely populated interior regions of Australia.

Photosynthesis The process by which plants use sunlight to make energy-rich food from carbon dioxide and water, releasing oxygen.

Plateau A relatively flat-topped upland landform.

Population structure The numbers and proportion of people in particular age-groups within a given population.

Productivity The output achieved from a certain level of resource use, investment and effort.

Quota A form of control or rationing that states a limit, for example the amount of wheat a farm may produce in a year.

Refugee A migrant who has been forced to flee from his/her country.

Regeneration The revival of a declining area.

Salination An unhealthy build-up of natural salts in the surface of the soil.

Savannah A dryland ecosystem dominated by grassland with scattered trees and bushes.

Semi-arid A term used to describe an environment that generally receives 250–400mm annual rainfall.

Specialisation The concentration on one or a small number of products or services.

Subsidy A contribution of money, especially one made by a government to support a project.

Tablelands Relatively flat-topped uplands, usually edged with steep, descending slopes.

Tariff A tax on imports, intended to protect local products.

Temperate Usually refers to climates without great extremes of heat or cold.

FURTHER INFORMATION

BOOKS TO READ:

Eyewitness Travel Guides: Australia (Dorling Kindersley Publishing, 2003) Illustrated reference.

Fodor's Explore Australia 2003 (Random House Inc, 2004). Comprehensive illustrated guidebook.

Lonely Planet Australia by Paul Harding (Editor), 11th Edition (Lonely Planet Publications, 2002) Comprehensive illustrated travel guidebook.

Lizard Island: Science and Scientists on Australia's Great Barrier Reef by Sneed B., III Collard (Franklin Watts Books, 2000) A narrative study of marine life on the Great Barrier Reef, set at Lizard Island Research Station.

The National Geographic Traveler: Australia by Roff Martin-Smith (AA Publishing, 1999) A comprehensive guidebook with visitor tips, maps and environmental and historical information.

The Rough Guide to Australia (Rough Guides, 2003) Comprehensive travel guidebook.

WEBSITES:

GENERAL INFORMATION ON AUSTRALIA:

www.csu.edu.au/australia
www.odci.gov/cia/publications/factbook/geos/as.html
www.australiangeographic.com/index.cfm
www.gov.au (Government website)
www.dfat.gov.au/geo/australia (Factsheets)
www.abs.gov.au (Statistics)
www.dpie.gov.au (Agriculture)
www.erin.gov.au (Environment)

ABORIGINAL CULTURE:

www.aboriginalaustralia.com
www.aboriginalart.com.au
www.nlc.org.au

TOURIST INFORMATION:

www.australia.com
www.atn.com.au
www.about-australia.com
www.greatbarrierreef.aus.net

FILM:

Rabbit Proof Fence Directed by Philip Noyce (Rated PG, released 2002; available on video and DVD, 2003) Based on the true story of three aboriginal girls and their struggle for freedom in 1930s Australia.

JOURNALS:

Australian Geographer (Journal of the Geographical Society of New South Wales, published quarterly)

Australian Geographical Studies (Journal of the Institute of Australian Geographers, also quarterly)

USEFUL ADDRESS:

Australian High Commission
Australia House
The Strand
London WC28 4LA

Numbers shown in **bold** refer to pages with maps, graphic illustrations or photographs.

A shingleback or stumpy-tailed lizard, one of Australia's unique reptile species.

Pink mulla mullas and snappy gums at the Millstream-Chichester National Park in Pilbarra, Western Australia.